Advance Reviews for
Signs in the Dark

Young adults who choose Signs in the Dark for either its intrigue or its insights into a deaf girl's world are in for a wild ride in a multifaceted thriller that holds solid action and emotional revelations throughout. – D. Donovan, Senior Reviewer, Midwest Book Review

Susan Miura is an exceptional author who creates intriguing characters from different backgrounds and ethnicities in all her books. She also does a phenomenal job of introducing readers to unique topics through her engaging stories. This novel touches on human trafficking, wildlife conservation, hearing impairment, abandonment, and overcoming pains from the past. I've thoroughly enjoyed all of her YA books, but *Signs in the Dark* is my favorite. – Leslea Wahl, young adult author and recipient of the Moonbeam, Readers Favorite, & Illumination book awards.

Signs In The Dark captivated me from the first page. Susan Miura's story-telling chops are powerful and polished. Her characters, Haylie, a deaf and courageous young woman, and Nathan, who has more than a casual interest in her, are so real and appealing that it's impossible to stop reading. A must-read for young (and mature) adults. I can't wait for her next novel. – Libby Hellmann, best-selling crime author and host of the Second Sunday Books podcast.

Other books by Susan Miura

Healer Series
Healer
Shards of Light

Pawprints in the Snow

SIGNS IN THE DARK

SUSAN MIURA

For my amazing family and friends,
who illuminate my world like brilliant stars,
and for those in the Deaf Community who inspired this story.

Chapter 1

Haylie
Wednesday Night

A squad car flashes red and blue as it races down the street, its siren swallowed by silence. Just like the fireworks bursting over Navy Pier. Music. Thunder. Voices. Sounds that will never be my reality, and yet...being deaf has its advantages. People think I have a sixth sense, but it's just a matter of noting the shift in a person's eyes, the prickle of electricity in the air when a storm is miles away. No storms ride the breeze in this alley tonight, though; there's just me and that fat harvest moon, illuminating the autumn sky like a cosmic jack-o-lantern and whispering a silent warning that creeps along my spine and lingers at the base of my neck.

Something's wrong. Nathan should have been here by now. My eyes scan the alley one more time before I reread his text.

Need to talk. Can you meet me in 10 behind your garage?

Unexpected, but then, I have no point of reference for what to expect. I take a mental tally of what I know. He's a swimmer, with a nice smile and dark eyes that look at me like I'm...someone special. He's Latino, I think. And he's friends with that soccer guy everyone thinks is so hot. He seems to be doing okay in our physics class, so he's got some brains. And I've seen him from across the lake, playing with his dogs in the backyard – extra points for that. Not much to go on, and yet...there's something about him. Something that makes me excited for our date on Friday.

Movement by the gate startles me. I jump, too on edge from standing in the darkness alone, then see my little brother heading toward me with something flopped over his arm.

"Mom says it's cold." Ben signs better than any hearing person I know. He holds up the hoodie I bought last week when Kamiko and I spent the day in Chicago. I happily put it on, remembering how I almost left it under the seat on the Metra train.

Instead of heading back down the gangway, Ben stays put, scrunching up his nose as he sniffs the air around us. "What's that smell? It's the same one I smelled when we were hiking in Brazil. Remember? That day we saw the anaconda and Mom freaked out?"

A fun memory, though I was happy to put some distance between us and that terrifyingly beautiful snake. I ponder whether to answer Ben's question about the familiar sweet, earthy aroma that often lingers in the alley when the breeze carries it from our neighbor's yard. "Nothing. Somebody must have been cooking." Mom or Dad can explain weed to him. He doesn't need to know tonight.

"It's stinky." He attempts to wave away the scent with his hand, which makes me laugh, but we both stop and squint as a car turns into the alley, catching us in its headlights. It stops, pauses, and backs out onto the street.

"That was weird," Ben says.

I nod, wondering if it was Nathan. Would Ben's presence cause him to leave?

"You got a package right after you went out." He climbs the low fence separating the alley from our yard and perches on top. "It's a little one from your original dad."

"Okay. Thanks." Ben's name for my bio father makes me smile, but really, what else would he call him? It must have been strange finding out Mom was married before and I'm only his half-sister. He never even questioned the difference in our skin color – mine milky white and his mocha latte, until the conversation a few months ago. There's nothing "half" about it to me and Ben, though. We're all in, for better or for worse, through thick and thin, the whole enchilada and all the other clichés.

"When can I meet him?" Hopeful eyes peer at me through the darkness. He hates feeling left out.

The answer eludes me. It's only been two months since my father re-entered my life. We've got a lot to unpack. Having him meet Ben isn't a priority. Not yet. I look at my brother, with his sugar plum heart ready to trust anyone, and want to place him in a bubble where no one can ever break him. He doesn't know what it's like to get left behind. To carry a dark, bitter load of hurt and hate. That will never be part of his world. Not while I'm alive.

"I want to get to know him better first, okay? So it might be awhile. Sorry, kiddo."

"Don't call me that. I'm not a kid anymore."

The intensity in those eight-year-old eyes makes me want to laugh, but I stifle it, knowing my little brother is sensitive. "Sorry."

"He's nice, right?"

Ben thinks that's an easy question. He waits for me to say "yes" because my father's been "nice" for the past two months, but there's about fourteen years of radio silence to consider. The occasional birthday or Christmas card only served as painful reminders that he walked out on me and Mom when I was three. A girl can't just let that go.

"He visits you and texts you and bought that big stuffed bunny."

All true. All good. Cutest bunny ever. And yet, after

each visit, I wonder if it will be our last. "It's complicated. Give it some time, okay? And go back inside."

"Why do *you* get to have two dads?"

His words imply I won the lottery. As if there weren't a hundred nights I laid in bed wondering what I did to make my father go away. And when I got older, a hundred more wondering how he could choose gambling over me and Mom. Over his job. Over *everything*. Because in the end, that's what he lost. Ben doesn't get it. He's the lucky one. The dad we share, who loved me enough to adopt me when my bio father signed away his rights, would never leave us.

"Just go back inside. Please. We'll talk about it later. Go play Pokémon with Dad."

"He's not back from Wild Things yet. One of the tigers has a tooth infection. I think it was Fang. Or maybe Mika. Yeah, Mika. Anyway, I like it here. Look at the moon. It's so big and orange."

No wonder Mika's eating has been off the past couple of days. I take comfort in knowing our beautiful Bengal is in good hands with the best wildlife vet in the business. She sure wasn't in good hands before she came to our rescue center. At least now she can live in peace, with room to roam. My eyes return to the mesmerizing moon. "It's gorgeous, but you still need to go. I'm meeting someone." My words hold far more optimism than my heart.

"Who?"

"A guy from my class." I'm done answering questions, but there's no doubt in my mind that Ben's not done asking them.

He wraps his arms around himself in a body hug and makes a kissy face.

Chances are slim he can see my eye roll through the veil of night, but I do it anyway. "Go in. I'm serious." His stupid kissy face might have been funny some other time, but not when I'm feeling like an idiot for waiting out here. I turn away, but his tug on my sleeve brings my attention back to him.

"Who's that guy on the phone?" He points down the alley, behind me.

My head whips around to see the glow of a phone illuminating a face that isn't Nathan's. Must be someone from the neighborhood just needing a little privacy for a call. He turns his back to us and walks away.

"No one. A neighbor. Go *now*, Benjamin. My friend will be here any second."

"Fine." He stomps the entire way down the sidewalk to let me know he's offended.

I look at my phone again, which makes no sense, but neither does standing in this stupid vacant alley. It clearly says *10*. My *yes* got sent, so Nathan must know I'm here. Twenty-five minutes of wondering what's going on makes me think he's cancelling Friday's pizza date. It would have been nice to see if he was really as smart and funny and decent as he seems. To be close to him somewhere other than a classroom, where hands might touch. Or lips. To get lost in the depths of those ebony eyes that draw me in like an unmarked path in the rainforest. But if he needs to talk, it's probably not going to happen. Maybe I was wrong about him.

His loss.

Wind scatters gold and crimson leaves along the fences and garage doors as I zipper my hoodie to the top. Two more minutes, that's it. Mr. Nathan Boliva is about to get a message stating very clearly he can forget about Friday. If this is how he treats girls, he's definitely not the guy for me. Still, that nagging feeling remains. Something's wrong. My eyes are drawn to the sky again, where black clouds drift in front of the moon, shadowing the alley into a darker shade of dark, and channeling a thought as undeniable as it is unexplainable.

The something wrong isn't Nathan.

Vibrations emerge from behind me, followed by

familiar waves of warmth. A car. With no headlights. In a dark alley. Too cliché for a horror flick, and yet...here it is. And I know it's real because my adrenaline just leaped into overdrive. Phone Guy runs toward me. Hope rises. He'll help, or at least call the police. But there's something weird about his face. The shape is off. No features emerge through the darkness.

An ogre hand clamps over my mouth, jerking my head backward toward a silver coupe. Phone Guy reaches me, close enough for me to see his black ski mask. It obscures his face, but not the creepy eyes that glare rivers of terror through my heart. Did Nathan do this? Why? I'm nearly to the car door. I can't let them get me inside. Staying alive and out of that car are my only goals.

Wide shoulders, thick arms; they're definitely men. Screams quiver my flimsy vocal cords, their sound blocked by a salty, sweaty hand. They've pinned my arms, but my feet strike out in every direction. From the shallow front pocket in my jeans, my cell crashes to the ground.

There goes my lifeline.

My right foot lashes out frantically and strikes a shinbone. My fingers find flesh and dig in like tiger claws, but in the end, these small victories matter little. Despite my best efforts, the whole grab-n-go takes seconds. Rough hands shove me into the car's back seat.

Now they can take me anywhere; do anything. *Anything.*

This battle is lost, but the war is on. These guys are about to find out there's plenty of fight left in me and I'll use it until my last breath, which may come sooner than I ever imagined. I picture Mika, strongest tigress at the shelter, and try to channel her power. Her aggression. Nobody messes with Mika. That's who I need to be right now.

The faceless demon shoves a rag between my lips with pudgy fingers I try to bite. Instead, I catch my lip, which bleeds into the rag. Its sickening, metallic taste churns my stomach, but that's the least of my problems as they expertly flip me face down on the seat and bind my wrists. Plastic ties cut into my skin. I struggle to break free, kicking the door, the window, anything, but in half a heartbeat they've got my ankles bound, too.

Deaf, voiceless, and almost completely immobile. The tiger in me has been conquered. For now. An icy wave of despair sweeps through my body. The driver reaches back and hands something to the guys who hold me down. From the corner of my eye, I glimpse a syringe.

Oh, God!

I send up desperate pleas to heaven, but no angelic armies swoop down to block their escape. No knights in shining armor or fairy godmothers materialize to save the day. Instead, a sharp pinch in my upper arm sends my panic soaring to a higher level, knowing who-knows-what is streaming through my veins. And as the car speeds off into the darkness, even my sixth sense fades in the face of a black tidal wave.

———

We're in a motel room. A dreamy, hazy motel room with a musty smell, peeling paint, and no bedding on the mattresses. I should be terrified. My heart should be pounding like a thousand drums. But I am calm. Limp. Subdued by the liquid serenity they injected into me. Indifferent to the mixed messages in my head saying "this is bad," and simultaneously "all is well." One of my captors carried me in. I laugh, thinking I probably looked like a drunk girl on a raunchy date with two masked men, but that's not funny at all. It's sad. That poor girl. But that poor girl is me, and there was no one around to see me. So dark out there. No lights. Where did the moon go? Such a big beautiful moon. I want to ask them if they saw it, but my hands are tied.

The shorter guy cuts my ankle ties and guides me to a

chair. It is stiff. Wooden. Probably a desk chair. He eases me into it and a little voice inside whispers "Fight, Haylie. Fight!" But my body does not respond.

I'm reluctantly complacent as they remove my shoes and rearrange the ropes, winding them around my torso to secure me to the back of the chair. This is not me. There's still a me inside that wants to bare my claws and fangs, but that message isn't reaching my arms and legs. My attempt to scream fails miserably, with little more than a pathetic puff of air emerging from my lungs.

An hour goes by. Maybe. It's impossible to tell for sure in this dreamy state of mind, but it feels like an hour. The fog is beginning to lift from my brain. Shifting air and vibrations beneath my feet tell me the men are moving around, but no one has touched me. Maybe that's good. But the words "human trafficking" keep haunting me, and I can't help wondering if this is my first stop on a journey into my darkest fears.

Chapter 2

Nathan
Thursday afternoon

"So, there's this girl." I almost laugh at the memory of saying that to Cougar and Ruby last week. Almost. Their goofy butterfly ears perked, waiting to hear the word "treat," then slumped again as I described how her wavy hair drapes down her back and reminds me of summer wheat. I even used signing to tell them she's deaf, just because I need the practice, and that I saw her in the bleachers at my last swim meet. Two sets of Greyhound eyes followed my awkward hand movements as I formed the words...or what *might* have been the words. Thankfully, dogs don't judge. Or question. Or mock. I tossed them each a Pup Crunch and told them what I'd *never* tell my friends; that she's spring rain and fireworks and sunrise and storms all rolled into one.

But none of that compares to the most important thing about the girl I should be sharing a pizza with tomorrow night. Because the most important thing about Haylie, at least for now, is that she's missing.

"Are you *absolutely sure* you have no idea where she is?" The middle-age FBI agent, Alessio, leans forward, her words probing, but not accusing. We've been hanging out for nearly two hours now; first at the house, where they were waiting when I got home from school, then in this CSI-style room, complete with two-way mirror, wall phone, and air left over from the 1960s. "Think about it. Take your time. Maybe something will come to you."

The only thing coming to me is the acid churning in my stomach, which I haven't felt since last spring when everyone was counting on me to win the hundred-meter Butterfly at Nationals. Which went much better than this.

"No, I told you. The police asked all these same questions last night. I *don't know*." They really don't get it. If I knew, I wouldn't be able to tell them fast enough. "Check at Wild Things, that wildlife rescue place. Her stepdad's the head of something. She hangs out there sometimes, helping with the animals." It's the only place that comes to mind, since what I know about Haylie could hardly fill a postcard. That was all supposed to change tomorrow night. "Maybe something weird happened." I rub clammy hands on my jeans, hoping they don't notice. Wishing I was anywhere but this stuffy room.

"As in?"

"Maybe an animal hurt her. They've got gorillas and tigers over there. Lions and some other things, too, I think. Maybe she can't yell. It's worth checking out, right?" My words pour out on a stream of adrenaline. Fast. Choppy. Saturated with guilt for a crime I didn't commit. And if I sound guilty to *me*, I can only imagine what these agents are thinking. Images of prison pummel my brain – steel bars, strip searches, the option to join a gang or die. But the fear is fleeting as I circle back to Haylie and wonder, as my heart continues to race, whether hers is beating at all.

Agent Alessio sighs. Kind eyes gaze at me like I'm a wounded creature caught in a bear trap. "Nathan, you realize you are not under arrest and you can leave any time, right?"

Two problems with that. One, Dad would kill me. He

wants me to cooperate with them, even though it's a waste of time.

"Peruvians do the right thing," he'd said. "Go. Answer their questions. Be respectful. Make me proud."

And two, not cooperating would make me look guiltier, if that's even possible. She waits for me to nod my understanding.

"We just want information that will lead us to Haylie," she continues. "Anything. Would you like your parents to join us? Or perhaps an advocate?"

"A what?"

"An adult who will look out for you; make sure your rights are not being violated."

I sit up straighter. "I'm fine." I force a tone of resolve into my voice, hoping to convince myself as well as them. Part of me loves the idea of having someone here who knows what's going on. Someone with experience who's on my side. A swim coach for criminal suspects who didn't do anything criminal. But in a few weeks, I'll be old enough to vote for the leader of our country, apply to college, start the path toward becoming a firefighter. Lots of decisions and challenges on the horizon. Time to step up. "I'm fine." Repeating the phrase seems like a good way to emphasize my decision, but the tiny wrinkles on Agent Alessio's forehead tell me she's not convinced.

She nods and turns toward her partner—some kind of silent cue that it's his turn to ask more questions I can't answer. I switch my gaze to a guy whose blond buzz cut reminds me of the neo-Nazi group that held a rally in Daley Plaza last month. He glares at me with unblinking snake eyes, if snake eyes were watery gray, in a melodramatic attempt to be intimidating. Maybe it's a good-cop-bad-cop routine. Or maybe he's just that guy.

"Where's your cell phone, Nate?"

Nate. Like he knows how much that grates me. Nate is fine...for guys who go by Nate. I'm Nathan. The whole world calls me Nathan. Except this Smirley guy. And my phone? He knows the answer. He knows everything I told the cops last night.

"Gone. Which is what I told the police. Stolen yesterday. I am *not* the one who sent her that text about meeting in the alley."

"Explain how it got stolen. And yes, I know you told the police. Now tell *us*." Suspicion saturates every word.

Hidden beneath the table, my hands clench and release. I tell them it got taken from Alec's car when we were practicing goal kicks at the park. Well, *he* was. I just stood in the goal, failing to block most of them and wishing my best friend had joined me on swim team. "When we got back to his car, my phone was gone." But under the florescent light and the weight of Smirley's glare, that very true story sounds phony, even to me.

"Your phone gets stolen the same day Haylie disappears." His eyes narrow to slits. "And yet, Haylie received a text message from you yesterday at 6:42 p.m."

"I know, I know. Ask the police about it. They checked with Alec last night."

"The English boy?"

"Yeah." No doubt they thought his accent was cool. Everyone does. At least, every living, breathing female. "He told them the same thing."

Smirley clicks his pen five irritating times. "Did you file a police report on the *stolen* cell phone?"

"No, sir." I answer quickly, knowing I reek of guilt more with every pause. "Alec didn't lock the car." I told him to lock it, but he called me "barmy" and said nobody would want his old rusty beater, so why bother? *Thanks, Alec.* "I figured the police had more to do than search Heron Lake Village for my missing phone. Probably shouldn't have left it on the car seat."

Agent Alessio sits down. "You have to understand how serious this is, Nathan. We have people out looking for Haylie right now, but at the moment, you're our best source of information. Something that might seem repetitive or inconsequential to *you* may actually provide a useful clue for *us*."

I nod. Her calm demeanor steadies my breathing, but it will likely be short lived as Smirley leans forward to speak again.

"Tell us about meeting Haylie, even if you told the police."

This was hard enough to go through once. Can't believe I'm on round two. I suppress a sigh, knowing attitude will just drag this out longer. "I'd wanted to talk to her for a while, but I guess I didn't know what to say." Warmth creeps up from the acid pit and floods my face. Even *I* can tell how lame that sounds.

Smirley scribbles some notes. "Do you have a problem talking to people? Do you have friends, or do you spend a lot of time alone?"

Clearly, he sees me as a social outcast, talking to other crazies in chat rooms and Googling ways to make bombs or homemade poison. Shifting in my seat, I wonder how to tell these suits about how pretty she is, how smart, how classy. Instead, I lean forward and meet his gaze, no easy task with visions of Haylie in my head...and all the things that could be happening to her while I answer stupid questions. "Yes, I have friends. I was just a little shy around Haylie. Probably because of the signing." I reach for the glass of water they gave me, mostly for something to do. "We all learn to sign at school. Well, not the deaf kids, they already know how, but the hearing kids have to take classes. I'm not the greatest at it."

"And she's your classmate and also your neighbor?"

Another nod. "We're in Physics together. She's not my neighbor, exactly. We both live on Heron Lake, but she's on the other side."

Our backyards face each other from opposite banks, which I didn't know 'til I met her in class and saw her walking out of her house a few days later. Black shorts. White crop top. Ponytail swinging as she went for a run.

Agent Smirley's chair scrapes against the floor as he stands. The sound snaps me back to the present...and the harsh reality that comes with it.

"So what changed? How and when did you make plans with her?"

Agent Alessio takes off her glasses and they both look at me, but my mind is whirling through the scene, editing and deleting personal details. I'm not going to explain that first Alec caught me waving to her and harassed me mercilessly when he found out that had been the extent of our two-week communication. Once the harassment ended, he moved on to his third favorite thing: giving me advice. Slots one and two were taken up by soccer and girls.

"Blimey, Nathan, you can't just go around waving for the rest of your life." He shook his head like there weren't words powerful enough to reflect his disappointment. "If you fancy her, ask her out. And don't go to Café Luis again. Try someplace different for once in your life."

That's how Alec rolls. No wisecracks about the challenges of dating a deaf girl; just move forward. Do something. Grab a vine and leap.

"Okay, okay, I'll ask." Saying it out loud gave me the guts to actually do it.

Smirley opens his mouth to say something that will surely be annoying, so I cut him off.

"I gave her a note on Tuesday. Asked if she wanted to walk over to Italian Village for pizza after school on Friday." Which is where we would have been tomorrow night. Talking, eating, trying to communicate in our different languages and not caring if it was awkward. Maybe even ending with a kiss. At least, that's what I'd hoped.

"Then what?" Alessio asks.

"She gave me one back. She said 'yes' and to meet her by the Beethoven statue." My monotone words don't begin to reflect the pounding of my heart in that moment.

She had smiled and walked down the hall, that silky hair swaying across her back like an amber wave and me grinning like I'd just won Olympic gold...until I remembered my pathetic signing skills. I tried to imagine our conversation, hoping I wouldn't attempt to ask what kind of pizza she wanted, and instead sign "your grandma is hot." My determination to avoid that disaster meant lugging my ASL book home the next few nights.

"Anything else?"

"Nothing major. Nothing that's gonna help find her. We exchanged a few texts and notes. That's it."

He pulls a familiar piece of paper out of his briefcase and slides it in front of me. "Like this one?"

My eyes scan the words I'd written yesterday, just hours before she disappeared.

I'll meet you by Beethoven tomorrow. As for Saturday—watch out. I'll be armed and dangerous. -- Nathan

My entire body cringes. Every muscle. Every organ. Every hair. "We both signed up for a laser tag thing this Saturday at school. We were joking around about it. You know, joking around. Just...

"Yes, we get it. *Joking.*"

"It's okay, Nathan." Alessio gives Smirley a sideways glance. Quick, but its meaning is clear. "Tell us about the note."

"It said 'No mercy on Saturday.' And she signed it 'Three-time champion at Windy City Laser World.' She underlined the word 'champion.' Twice. It's in my locker. I'll get it for you."

"No need. We've got it." Smirley turns down the sarcasm, but there's no erasing the smug from his face.

I pretend to suppress the humiliation of them searching my locker, just because I know he'd love to see me rattled, but there's no hiding the red heat burning in my cheeks. "So I sent *this* one."

Agent Alessio recaps the story, finishing with the

stolen phone. I begin to relax in my less-than-comfortable wooden chair, figuring this endless session might actually be ending.

"Keep going with your story, Nathan. Everything that happened next."

There is nothing about the next few hours that will help their investigation. I'm sure of it. It was a meatloaf and potatoes kind of day, smothered in normal.

"I went back home, finished my English paper, and took Cougar, my dog, for a run down the lake path. When we got back, my mom had just returned from volunteering at the Greyhound Rescue Center. She asked me to go buy cilantro for the aji." I'd asked her if she could make the aji without it, but she looked at me like I'd suggested we eat hazardous waste.

Smirley scrunches his face, like he breathed in fertilizer. "Aji?"

"It's Peruvian hot sauce, Carl." Agent Alessio jumps in before I can answer. "Really quite good. Spicy, too." She turns back to me. "So you went to the store?"

"Yeah. Elena's Mart over on Maple." The store is in the opposite direction of Haylie's house, but I cruised past it anyway; a little detail I choose to omit. Seems to me I've already offered up a lifetime's worth of personal disclosures. It was that shadowy time of night, when everything looks kinda blue, and there was this huge moon hanging in the sky. I drove down her block, then turned back toward the store. It seemed inconsequential at the time, but now I wonder if I could have prevented whatever happened. I should have knocked on the door and talked a few minutes. She would have known I didn't have my phone. Didn't text her. Instead, I went to Elena's Mart and bought cilantro.

An hour later, she was gone.

Smirley's eyes seem to peer through mine and into my brain, where I'm sure he's searching for the missing part of my story. "What do you know about the ransom note?"

My thoughts...and breath...screech to a stop. I try to process the words. *Ransom note.* My memory searches for any reference to a ransom note. Nothing. How is it possible they never mentioned it 'til now? It makes no sense. Haylie's not rich. Not that I know of, at least. "What are you talking about?"

"This one." Smirly slides the paper across the table, replacing the note with my lame attempt at humor. "This is the reason the FBI got involved." Four sentences printed off a computer jump off the page and claw my heart.

We have Haylie. If you want to see her again, don't call the cops. We'll contact you with further instructions. We are armed and ready to do whatever's necessary.

His eyes narrow, darkening to slate gray. "Interesting, don't you think? Especially that part about being armed and ready?" He taps my note to Haylie, but his gesture is meaningless compared to the images assaulting my brain.

Haylie captive. Someone grabbing her, hurting her, tying her up. I try to breathe, but all the air's been sucked out of the room. And somewhere in the midst of this whirlwind, his words sink in. *Armed and ready.* My new role as suspect becomes clear as pool water. Could they possibly think my lame attempt at being funny was related to the ransom note?

"Haylie's a pretty girl. I'm thinking...maybe you just wanted her all to yourself."

Red flags shoot up in my brain, waving wildly as I wonder where he's going with that. No place good, for sure.

Smirley sits, his face inches from mine. "And just maybe, once you had her, you thought it might be a great way to make some money, too. Maybe go to a university instead of community college. Buy yourself a car. I get it."

"I didn't want her all to myself. Or money. I just asked her out for pizza."

"Come on now, Nate. I'm only twelve years older than

you. I remember what it's like. You're what, ten days or so from turning eighteen?"

He looks at me all friendly like, as if we're about to share a little secret.

"Admit it. You've probably fantasized about being alone with Haylie, having her at your beck and call, there whenever you want her. I mean, who wouldn't? Pretty face, nice body, and the best part is...she doesn't talk."

My heart hammers my chest. My hands clench the edges of the chair, aching to clench his throat instead. "*What?*" I force the word out between gritted teeth, my voice emerging louder, higher than usual. He's baiting me, but knowing it doesn't stop the anger that swoops through my brain in a flash of heat, clouding my reasoning and vision. "Are you *insane*?" When my eyes clear, I see Alessio wince like she'd just gulped spoiled milk. But Smirley doesn't seem to notice.

"All right, kid!" His volume rises with each word. "I'm asking you flat out!" He morphs from milky white to lava red in seconds, glaring at me like I've got Haylie chained to a wall in a crawl space under my house. His hand slaps the table. "WHERE IS HAYLIE SUMMERS?"

His tirade replaces any remnants of my fear with uncensored rage. "I have no idea!" I smack the table, Smirley style, wanting to call him every name running through my head, but force myself to stop. For Haylie. Only for Haylie. I need to get out of here. Need to find her. And telling this moron what he can go do with himself will only keep me here longer.

Smirley stands, points at me. "I want to know—"

"Excuse us, Nathan," Alessio butts in. "We'll be right back." She looks at Smirley and gestures toward the door. Before they close it behind them, Smirley glances at his partner and asks, "What's goin' on, Amy?"

A few minutes alone settles my pulse back to almost normal. Clears my head enough to figure out a plan. I need to stay calm and answer their questions so this nightmare can end. I need to get home. Search for Haylie. Give Ruby her meds. It's way past time for her pill and she's probably feeling the pain. When the door opens again, only Alessio walks through, holding a bag of chocolate chip cookies from the vending machine across the hall. She offers it to me, but I shake my head and keep my arms folded. She sets the bag on the table. "Calm down, Nathan."

Somewhere I heard eyes are the window to a person's soul. Smirley's smolder like wildfire smoke, but Alessio's are more like a forest.

"Agent Smirley didn't mean to get you angry. We're just trying to find the girl, and right now everybody's a suspect."

"Yeah, whatever." I reach for the bag and grab a cookie. At least she's not a maniac like her partner.

"Do you know anyone who'd want to kidnap Haylie?"

"No."

"Did Haylie seem upset about anything lately?"

"No, but we haven't talked much."

Alessio opens an envelope and pulls out a photo, setting it on the table in front of me. "Recognize this guy?"

The face staring back at me is ordinary enough; pleasant even. A fiftyish guy, black skin, brown curly hair cut short and tinged with gray. Glasses. Small mole or birthmark on his temple. I search my memories, hoping I've seen him somewhere, but there's nothin'. I shake my head. She tells me it's Russell Summers, Haylie's stepdad, but her cell goes off before she can say anything more. After a few "uh-huhs" and a "be right there," she taps it off.

"My apologies. Be right back." She disappears, leaving me with nothing but a question that echoes repeatedly, until it becomes a mantra. How did this happen?

I scan the beige walls for anything of interest. Anything to take my mind off this nightmare. Too bad Alec isn't here. Talking to him would ease the anxiety that's tearing away at my gut. He'd sit in that chair across from me, laughing at the absurdity of "the whole bloomin' thing." But the chair remains vacant, its cold metal frame mocking my desire for companionship. It's just me and the two-way mirror. Is there a bad guy on the planet who would think it's just a mirror? I glance at it, wondering if they're watching, and see an exhausted, stressed-out version of me. Tawny skin, swimmer's body, still two inches shorter than Alec's six-foot frame. Still wishing I could turn time back to a few months ago, when everything made sense. Before Alec started disappearing on Saturday afternoons. Before the vet told me about Ruby's sickness. Before Haylie disappeared into the night.

Agent Alessio returns, holding my laptop. I'm too short on optimism to hope that's a good sign.

"Your story checked out in separate conversations with Alec and your parents. Your laptop looks clean, and the ransom note didn't come from your printer." She hands the laptop back to me. "You're free to go. We'll be in touch."

I sigh, feeling like I've been holding my breath for two hours. Alessio seems okay. I guess she's just doing her job. She smiles and hands me her card as the door opens and Smirley saunters back in.

"Stick around town 'til this is settled," he says.

"Yes, sir." His command hits my mental garbage file as the words leave my mouth. I resist the urge to bolt out the door, walking at a normal pace toward the waiting area. Haylie is missing. Beautiful, brilliant, sweetheart Haylie. And I'm going to find her. Whatever it takes. Wherever it takes me.

Chapter 3

Haylie
Thursday, Early Evening

I'm back in the chair, having spent the night and most of the morning in bed with my brain on overdrive. The big guy, nearly the size of a grizzly bear, just replaced the younger guy in jeans. He pulls off the blindfold and cuts the ties, which means it's time for another meal break. Grizzly faces me, wearing that ghoulish ski mask that might not be disturbing on a ski slope, but in this grungy, dismal motel room, it still creeps me out. His scraggly salt-and-pepper beard extends past the mask, revealing a vaguely familiar patch of white on the left side. The scent of his cologne reaches into my subconscious, trying to grab an elusive memory. We've met. Maybe only once, briefly, but somewhere tucked away too deep for me to grasp is an encounter with this guy.

Man, he's big. I don't know what I'll do if...no, I can't go there.

As he opens the paper bags on the table, a food aroma overtakes his cologne, telling me hamburgers are on the menu again. My next move might result in no meal at all, but I'll take that risk. I mime a writing gesture, hoping he goes for it. He does, handing me a pen and a yellowed motel notepad bordered with the words *Sunset Inn.* Now I know where I am, which is weirdly comforting, even if I've never heard of it. It's information I can give the cops if I escape. *When* I escape.

I write "vegetarian." He glances from the word to me to the bags, opens them, and unwraps the burgers. My empty stomach debates between hunger and eating meat, knowing I'm going to need strength to escape or fight them. Grizzly plucks off the top buns, along with the lettuce, pickles and cheese from both sandwiches, then lays my burger on top of his and replaces the bun. The rest of the toppings get piled onto my bun. Apparently, he believes this is now a vegetarian sandwich. Never mind that my "vegetarian" ingredients are saturated with all the meat juices and grease, and his giant paws touched every part of my food. Still, he's trying, which is probably way more than I'd get from most evil kidnappers. He scoots my chair up to the table and gestures for me to eat. I do, with my muscles relaxing for the first time since my abduction. Killers don't try to comply with meal requests.

Before diving into his double meat burger, Grizzly turns on the news - a welcome distraction after hours of darkness. After the usual political scandals, they show a minivan half submerged in a river, where police investigators examine the scene. I munch my altered sandwich, watching the reporter's lips as she says all three people in the van were rescued. Next up is a church shooting. People cry, reporters ask questions, and the camera pans to a closeup of the church steeple, with its cross dramatically outlined against the sky. In that moment, I forget where I am. My heart hurts for the victims and all the people who loved them. Grizzly flips through channels, zipping past a reality show, a soda commercial ...and me. I put down my sandwich and focus on the screen. He does the same. The subtext reads "Haylie Summers, 17-year-old Beethoven High School junior, missing since last night. Haylie is deaf. Police suspect foul play."

Haylie is deaf. Why did they add that? It's not what defines me. It's not what matters when someone is forcibly taken from their home. It's also a really irrelevant thing for me to be concerned with right now, but I can't help it.

My sophomore picture fills the screen. Bright smile, good hair day, purple sweater. The one I was wearing when Nathan asked me out. Grizzly stands and I freeze. As the reporter interviews my parents, he whips out his phone, pacing as he talks, eyes fixated on the TV. The pretty reporter holds the mic in front of Mom's face – a face drawn and ashen, eyes puffy, with no trace of her signature Starry Night eyeliner. She signs while speaking. "Please don't hurt my daughter," she says. "If you know anything, please come forward. I'm begging you." Her words shred my heart as she covers her face with her hands and turns away. Dad stares at the camera and signs, "We love you, Haylie. Be strong. We'll find you." He turns to comfort Mom.

Tension saturates the air, its weight bearing down on me like a blanket of fear. Grizzly's hand smacks the dresser. He stays on the phone, gesturing, pacing like a caged animal. I watch him with my muscles rigid as stone, wondering if I'll suffer the consequences of his anger and wishing I could read his lips through the mask. The story ends and he turns off the TV, hurling the remote and his phone onto the bed.

He's caught off guard, that much is clear. He must have thought the media, maybe even the police, wouldn't find out I was taken. I barely have time to ponder the thought before he slips on his shoes and jacket, tugging crazily at the sleeve caught on his watch. Completely flustered, he finally manages to unclasp his watch and lay it on the table, then replaces my ties and blindfold. Hands shaking, he clumsily gets me secured. It comforts me to know people are searching, even though that photo isn't going to help anyone find me when I'm tucked away in this motel. Grizzly's agitation makes me think they'll need to alter the game plan according to this new development. The current game plan, whatever it is, has left me unharmed. But as fear creeps back into my pours, I wonder how much that's going to change.

Vibrations from Grizzly's footsteps are easy to feel beneath my stockinged feet. It continues for several minutes, followed by the whoosh of cool air and the reverberation of the door closing. There is nothing to do but think. Mom and Dad aren't rich enough for this to be a money thing. Once again, the words *human trafficking* rip through my head like demon claws. I spent half the night wondering if they were planning to sell me in one of the hidden brothels that stain our country and so many others. I've read enough to know it happens to girls like me...even younger. Forced to be with a dozen or more men a night. Forced to do whatever disgusting thing they want. I shove away the horrific images, but they boomerang back. My stomach crunches in on itself. I fight the ties, determined to break free, but they only dig deeper into my skin. There must be some way to triumph over this captivity; some way to shock him with nothing but an empty room when he returns.

I bend my face and raise my shoulder, rubbing the blindfold against it. The only outcome of this tedious task is aching neck muscles and frustration born of futility. Until...a thin line of sight appears, motivating me to continue. My slit of vision widens. I tilt up my chin and see a desk with a landline teasing me from a few feet away. Ideas swirl around my head, fusing and forming into a plan. If I can hop the chair over to the phone, I can knock the receiver off with my chin and dial 911 with my nose. The dispatchers can tell where calls come from, so in theory, rescue is only minutes away. Very Hollywood, but it's all I have. Ben will love this story. By tonight, I'll be sitting on the couch telling him all about it, seeing his eyes widen, answering his million questions. And not minding one bit.

The first two hops inch me closer to my destination, but each takes more strength and agility than I'd imagined. Wobbling is an issue. Both times I straighten myself and prevent toppling to the floor. Next to the telephone, Grizzly's watch lays sideways on the desk, its backside etched with words I can't make out. The third hop gets me close enough to read it. "To Rob with Love, Mary." More knowledge to file away. Grizzly is Rob. And someone actually loves him. Mary. Such a sweet name. I'll bet Mary doesn't know he's a monster.

My plan is working. I'm nearly to the phone, I've semi-identified one of the bad guys, and freedom is just another chair hop away. Hope rises where moments ago it barely existed. Another hop, but the landing feels different. The wobbling is more intense. My pulse races as I strain every foot and ankle muscle in an attempt to stay upright. It sways to the left, to the right. My brain screams "nooo!" but the chair tumbles over.

I writhe and twist, determined to set myself free, but the ties win. There is *nowhere* to go from here. A tidal wave of despair crashes over me. Drops slide through the little opening in the blindfold and disappear into the worn beige carpet. And there, in that awkward position, mired in misery, my thoughts turn to my family.

Images of Mom crying wash through my head. Ben, too, with Dad's arms wrapped around both of them, maybe stroking their hair like he does with me whenever my world spins out of control. They must have their whole Bible study group praying like mad. My bio father must know by now, too. Maybe he'll be filled with regret that he lost out on all the years we could have been sharing life together. Maybe not. I picture Kimiko and my other friends from school and Wild Things calling our house, texting my parents, terrified of what the next update will bring. And poor Imani, she won't understand why "Girl" isn't coming to see her. I'm her best human friend. Hopefully, the other gorillas will comfort her.

Will I ever see my family and friends again?

Or Nathan? Confusion blurs my thoughts when his name forms in my mind. It was his text that put me in that alley. His action that placed me in the hands of the kidnappers. And yet...my heart still refuses to believe it. He's one of the good ones. I know it. It's written in the depths of his chestnut eyes. It's there in his shy smile. I can't be wrong. It is the last thought before falling asleep with my face smashed against the carpet.

———

A blast of cool air tells me someone has entered again. I stiffen, wondering each time the door opens if it's someone new. Someone whose intentions are worse than my captors. Through the little opening in the blindfold, all I can see are black shoes and dirty carpet. The chair is turned upright and a large sweaty hand clips the rope around my wrists. Fingers fumble with the blindfold, which drops to the floor. Light assaults my eyes. I squint as hazy shapes and colors materialize into objects and people. When my eyes finally focus, my heart stops its maniacal pounding and leaps out of my chest. Sweat comes from nowhere, instantly sticking clothes to skin.

I was better off blindfolded.

A steel gray gun points directly at my head, creating in me a new level of terror. I suck in a gasp and force my eyes beyond the barrel to see a masked man in a dark brown suit. He's still a mystery, but the masked face next to him isn't anonymous anymore. Grizzly Rob holds up a piece of paper with the words "don't scream," then points to the other guy's gun. Like that was necessary. I nod and make the same writing gesture I used before, determined to find out something, anything, about why I'm here.

The men face each other and must be discussing my request, based on their body language and slight hand movements. I ache for the ability to read those mask-covered lips, but it's simply impossible. Reading their hearts is easy, though, for they are black as the masks. Suit hands me a pen and the notepad. I manage to steady my hands enough to scratch off *vegetarian* and write *What do you want?*

He grabs the pen from me. *None of your business. Cooperate and don't scream.*

Yes, I got that. My eyes scan the men for details—more information to help the cops catch them. I ignore Grizzly, having already stored away my observations of him, and move to Suit. That gun, though. It unnerves me, so I cast my eyes downward and zero in on brown wingtipped shoes. A scuff mark scars the right side of the right shoe. The laces are round and shiny, like they're waxed, and there's a swirly design made of perforated dots. Filed away. My eyes shift to Grizzly, who's wearing a navy blue windbreaker I didn't see earlier. An embroidered gold racehorse, surrounded by a gold oval, decorates the pocket. I press these details into my memory, determined to recount each one when I am free.

Grizzly pulls out a cell and faces it toward me, while Suit grabs a paper from the desk and hands it to me.

> *Read the note below and sign the words. We are recording you. Do not say anything other than what's in the note. We will have this recording translated before sending it to your parents.*

He points from that part of the note to me and I nod my understanding. Suit walks toward me, stepping to the side of my chair and holding the gun inches from my temple so it shows in the recording. My racing heart is going to explode right out of my chest. And my hands. My shaking hands. Will they even get the signals from my brain, which could, at any moment, be blown into sticky bits all over this motel carpet? One press of the trigger. That's all it will take for me to be gone. Annihilated.

Grizzly jabs his finger toward the paper again. There is no time to be terrified. If I have any hope of surviving, I have to get it together long enough to communicate this message. I read it first, so there's no surprises, then freeze at the last line. My hands rise and begin. I have a job to do, and a metal barrel pointed at my head.

I am fine. I have not been hurt. Shaking hands form the words well enough for Mom and Dad to understand. *If you give them what they want, they will let me go unharmed. If not, they will kill me.*

I take a breath before signing the last word.

Slowly.

Chapter 4

Nathan
Thursday, Early Evening

My parents sit on the opposite side of the FBI waiting room, Dad's back to me. He crumples an empty bag of chips like he's trying to kill it. It must have been a pain, sitting in those metal folding chairs all this time. Four paper coffee cups rest on the table between them. Mom takes a sip from one, then glances up at the sound of my footsteps. She looks about ten years older than she did a couple of hours ago. My whole body sighs at the sight of them, weary eyes and all.

"Nathan." She stands up, steps toward me, her arms beginning to extend forward, but mine remain at my side. Not now. Not here. Not when all I want is to leave this place. Ruby's at home, hurting, and Haylie...I don't even know.

Mom remains in place, giving my arm a gentle squeeze, her eyes glistening. *"Como estás*? Are they done with the questions? Can we take you home?"

"I'm fine. And yeah, they're done."

Dad's chair scrapes the floor as he stands, too. His eyes lock on mine. He shakes his head. "You. *You*, of all people."

My mouth drops open as my heart takes the punch. He thinks I'm in on this? Nothing I just went through hit me like this unexpected and undeserved betrayal. He knows me better than that. He's *got* to. How could he --

Weathered hands pat my back. I flinch, then relax as he repeats it three more times like I'd just gotten a good report card. "The next thing you know, they will be questioning the Pope. Not that you are the Pope, do not get me wrong, *mijo*, but you surely had no part in this." He lowers his voice so only me and Mom can hear. "Anyone would be *loco* to think so."

Okay, that's better. Much better.

We get in the car and the grilling begins. What did the agents say? What did you say? Then what did they say when you said that? This isn't what I need right now, but they're so worried about me, I play along with it.

Once we get home, there's just two things I want to do, but Cougar dances frantically in front of me, making it clear I'm two hours late with his Pup Crunch. I toss him two, out of guilt, and grab Ruby's meds from the cabinet. She lifts her head from her dog bed, pain shadowing her eyes, and I hold out her pill, smothered in peanut butter. A few months ago, she would have gobbled it without even stopping to sniff. But that was then. "Come on, girl. Eat it. It'll take away the pain." She stares at me, sending a silent message I don't want to hear. The sleek red marbled fur along her neck is warm beneath my palm, but her protruding ribs make me wince. "Come on, Ruby," I whisper. "Please." I place the pill on her tongue and she reluctantly chews. "There you go. Good girl. You'll feel better soon."

"But only until it wears off."

I didn't realize Mom was listening.

She scoots down and scratches Ruby between her ears, then lifts her chin to look in her eyes. "*Mi niña hermosa.* Still beautiful with your fancy brindle coat." Ruby licks her hand, then lays her head back down. "You poor, sweet thing." Mom kisses Ruby's head, then heads to the kitchen to make her nightly cup of chamomile tea. "I know it's been a tough week, Nathan, but you must start thinking about—"

"Not tonight, okay? Can we just not talk about this tonight?" I didn't mean for it to sound harsh, especially after the night we've all had, but she caught me off guard. The topic of Ruby's demise is not something I can handle right now.

She sighs, shaking her head.

"Sorry. Just a little edgy tonight. I'm gonna go hit the rocks for a while." Imagining myself on the rocky bank of our lake is what helped me survive that interview. Peace and quiet. Moonlight and darkness. Somewhere to be alone with my thoughts. And fears.

Worry lines wrinkle her forehead, but I can tell she's easing up now that we're back on familiar turf. "It's so late, *mijo*. You should get some rest after all you've been through." There's something calming about hearing her say "my son" in Spanish. I guess because it means we are back in our own personal space, away from the strangers and stress. Away from the *policía* and *federales*.

Mom forces a smile and hugs me like I'm going away for a month. "Go. Be careful. It is very dark out there."

My sanctuary awaits. It's no Lake Michigan, but still, there's something cool about walking out your back door and having a little lake right there. The heron and his mate soar over their kingdom each morning. The white cranes feed along the shore. People parade down the path throughout the day, walking dogs, running, fishing. But at night...at night it's all mine. And that's the part I love. Just me and the moon and the water. I can sit on the rocks, swallowed up by the night, invisible to the world. It's where I can think. Focus. Sort things out. It's where I can talk to God without the world interfering.

I walk through our yard, glancing next door to old Mr. Kingman's arena of landscape perfection, but my eyes haven't yet adjusted to the darkness. Giant marigolds line the fence between our yards. Their orange and yellow blooms cast a bold scent that drifts on the night air. There is not a weed among them. He makes sure of that. He's probably in bed now, exhausted from a day of watering, trimming, and watching the world from his kitchen window. His life, day in and day out. It's a future I'm determined to avoid.

A short dirt path leads from our gate to the water's edge, where my "throne" awaits—a granite boulder, flattish on top, perfect for sitting and pondering life, which needs a lot of pondering at the moment. A nearly-full moon beams out from storm clouds, rippling a pathway of light in the water. Can Haylie see the moon? Is someone hurting her at this moment, while I sit here doing nothing? If all had gone according to plan, she would have been next to me on this rock in the next couple of days. Just us. Talking...or not. Gazing at the lake. Close enough to kiss.

I bow my head, knowing she needs a miracle. Nothing less will do.

Hey God, it's Nathan. A silent greeting, knowing He hears every thought.

Lightning flashes, illuminating the trees and water. Then darkness.

"Hey, Nathan."

I freeze. The voice comes from behind. I know God speaks to people, but I always thought it was an in-your-head kind of thing. A nudge or feeling. I turn to see Alec carefully choosing his steps over the rocks.

"Oh, it's you." I can't help smiling, despite everything. "I thought it was God."

"A lot of people make that mistake."

We laugh. It feels good, but only for a second. There's no reason for Alec to be out here this late. Not his thing.

"Mumster called." He nicknamed mom three years ago when he saw her wearing the friendly monster mask she sports every Halloween. "Thought you might fancy some company."

I shake my head. "You're kidding. And she sent *you* instead of Cat?"

"*Please.* My sister's so out of your league she's not even in eyesight. And in case you forgot, five years older." He holds up his hand, spreading out his fingers.

"Painfully true, on both counts." Cat's sea green eyes and long black hair are a killer combination. Every time she speaks with that heart-melting accent, my brain dissolves into oatmeal. She'll say, "Hey Nathan, what's going on?" and every time, *every single time*, I search my brain for a clever response and say "Um, nothin'."

"So, my criminal friend, you're stuck with *me.* Cat's not home much these days, anyway. Too much homework, I expect. Apparently, there's a lot of that with a master's. Seems I'm joining your 'only child' club."

He never mentions the other child; the one who died on his sixth birthday when he was still living in England. Ever since I've known him, Alec hates his birthday and barricades himself in his room all day. Doesn't even come to school, and definitely doesn't want to talk about it. "She died," he told me years ago. "It was an accident." I asked what happened, but he just repeated "accident," and that was that. Baby Jenna's sweet little face and big brown eyes stare out from a pink photo frame on the living room mantle, where she watches her family like a cherub frozen in time.

Alec sits down on a smaller rock next to the throne. "How you doin'?"

My gut clenches. "I'm good." I'm lying. He knows it. But it's what guys do; hide behind walls of false pretense thinking we look Marine Corps tough. I want to say this has been the worst day of my life, that the girl of my dreams is out there somewhere, maybe dead, maybe getting beaten or who-knows-what, and it's killing me. I *want* to, but I don't.

"Yeah?" He tosses a pebble into the lake and we watch the circular ripples move to the outer edges of the glowing water. A few geese honk, angered by our invasion of their territory. Another distant flash lights the lake. Alec waits.

"She's out there, Alec." I shift on my boulder so I can face him. "She could be hurt. This is insane. How could this happen?"

Alec shakes his head, searches the ground for another pebble. "I don't know. I've been asking that ever since Jenna died. Wish I could offer you more."

Everything comes back to the accident. Someday, I hope he lets down his walls enough to tell me what happened. But tonight...tonight has to be about saving Haylie. "What am I supposed to do, go to bed and hope they find her by morning? All those agents do is *talk*. They should be *out there*. Searching." My voice cracks. The lake blurs. I look down, hunting for answers among the rocks.

Alec finds a flat pebble and sends it sailing. Judging from the plops, it skips three times. "I guess they have to start somewhere. I mean, they can't search if they don't have information, right?" He hands me a smooth skipping stone and I whip it at the moonlight. "Come on, Nathan, this is the FBI we're talking about. Plus, the bobbies are trying to find her, too. They even had an Amber Alert on the telly. They'll find her."

I raise my eyes to meet his. "They're cops, not bobbies. And it's a *TV*. Speak English."

"*You* speak English."

This is normally where we laugh, but we just stare speechless at the lake, illuminated now and again by the lightning. No rain, just flashes from some far-off place. Loud, obnoxious honking from dozens of airborne geese breaks the quiet as they clumsily land with wings flapping and water splashing. This sets off the geese and ducks resting peacefully on the shore. In a heartbeat, our corner of the world erupts into an annoying upheaval of honks and quacks. Eventually, everyone settles down, with just a stray complaint. But the break in conversation is enough to let a plan creep into my brain. Agent Alessio kept asking me about the stepfather, Mr. Summers. He must be a suspect, too. What was his first name? Robert, Randall, Roland?

"Russell!" I blurt it out loud.

Alec looks up, eyes wide. "What?"

"Haylie's stepfather's name is Russell Summers. They kept asking me about him. Maybe we can check him out. You know, snoop around a little." My heart quickens. More action, less talking. That's what this investigation needs—someone actually *doing* something.

Alec's next pebble plops without even one skip. "You're getting a little bonkers here. We don't even know where he lives."

"Well, actually I do." He doesn't press me on this, and I'm grateful.

"Nathan, it's nearly eleven and there's school tomorrow. Where are we going to say we're going this late? My dad would flip. You know that."

Alec has a point.

"Then we sneak out. These are desperate times. Life and death. If we find out something that saves Haylie's life, it'll be worth it. Right?" I don't wait for him to answer. "We'll bike there. The car would be too loud. It's not that far. We'll check things out real quick and come right back."

A lone goose waddles our way as though intending to voice his opinion. He looks at me, honks once, and turns tail. Apparently, he doesn't support my plan. Alec sighs. I know that sigh. It means *I really don't want to do this, but I'll do it for you.*

"Lucky for you, you're my best mate." He shakes his head. "I'm probably going to get grounded because of a girl, and she's not even *my* girl. You suckered me in again,

Cristobal." Alec thinks my middle name is funny. I'm sure my grandfather, Abuelo Cristobal, wouldn't agree.

"I owe you one. Let's meet back here at midnight. Meantime, I'll Google the stepdad and pretend I'm going to bed."

"Don't forget, my dad gets up at 3:30 to open the bakery."

"No problem. We'll be back way before that. Promise." I start to stand up, but stop when I see that Alec remains firmly planted on the rocks, gazing out over the water.

"And I want something in return."

"Anything."

His gaze remains fixed on some invisible entity on the lake. "Quit interrogating me about Saturday afternoons."

Didn't see that coming. The fact that it's a bargaining tool proves my suspicions are right. And worse, his words make it clear: my suspicions must be tamer than the reality. "Years of telling each other everything, and you can't tell me where you go on Saturdays? It's been three weeks. If it was reversed, you'd be plying me with questions night and day."

"Not saying you're wrong; just saying that's my terms."

My shoulders slump. For the millionth time, my mind soars through a list of possibilities, always landing on drugs. Specifically, steroids. He's been bulking up lately. That's got to be it. Lost in my thoughts, I say nothing.

"You want company on this little adventure or not?"

Why do I feel like I'm making a pact with the devil? "Fine. I won't ask for three weeks."

"Five."

"Four."

"Deal. And when you ask again in a month, you'll get the same answer."

"Whatever. I get it." But I don't; I just want to get going.

We make our way back to the path and turn in opposite directions toward our houses. As I head to my room, Cougar shadows me. He plops down next to my bed with his shredded, one-eyed teddy bear, nuzzling it with that long black nose. A few inches away, Ruby whimpers in her bed, snout resting on the floor. She looks up at me with eyes deep and sweet as a pool of warm chocolate. But there's a sadness in those eyes that pills can't take away. I bend to kiss her head as Cougar continues to chew his demented bear, his black and white tail smacking the floor in a rhythmic pattern. They don't know our nightly routine will soon be disrupted by me sneaking out. Ruby won't say a word, but tattletale Cougar could easily ruin the plan.

My laptop awaits, still bearing the *"feliz cumpleaños!"* sticker from Uncle Renzo. Lucky for me, the popularity of his Café Peru translated into generous gifts to his favorite nephew. It hums itself on with a blue glow and transports a world of information to my fingertips. *All right, Google, show me your stuff.* A few finger taps are all I need to find Russell Summers. His name is highlighted on a list of websites from here to the Milky Way—websites you don't want your name connected with. Quite a resume there, Russell. Maybe it's a different guy. Or maybe Haylie's stepfather is a creep...and the very reason Haylie is missing.

Chapter 5

Nathan
Two Months Ago

The cute college tour guide flips her hair and smiles at Alec as we make our way toward the science hall. Of course she does. But it doesn't annoy me today. Nope, today is all about the future and my path to getting a fire science degree. These halls will lead me to smoke and flames, lights and sirens, rescuing people in danger. Not sure where these rooms will lead Alec, but he'll figure it out. Posters on the walls announce science club meetings, a study abroad program in Rome, a Wilderness Club. The stress I've felt about leaving high school dissipates as we tour the school and learn about its offerings.

"Quit grinning." He nudges me. "You look like a nerd. Since when are you excited about school?"

I breathe in the smell of college and the classrooms that will propel me into an exciting career. "This is different. Way better than high school."

We follow the group of twenty and enter a lab twice the size of the one at Beethoven High, with equipment I've never seen before. In the corner, a huge saltwater fish tank hums and glows. Clownfish, gobies, and small angels dart in and around the coral and sea plants.

"You hate 'different.' Admit it. You've wanted to be a firefighter since you were eleven. Never once considered another job." Alec ignores all the equipment and heads straight for the fish tank. "Every first date's at Café Louis, even though there's dozens of restaurants within fifteen minutes of our block. And have you *ever* tried an ice cream beside Moose Tracks?"

"I had Bear Tracks when we went to the Smokies."

"Literally the same exact ice cream. Oh, and blue shirts for school picture days. Always."

Maybe he'd like familiar things too, if he'd gotten dragged from here to there like I did. Sure, he left England and came to Heron Lake, but he didn't have to learn another language, or deal with kids mocking his accent. Just the opposite. And he didn't have to explain a thousand times that he wasn't from Mexico.

My mind journeys back to those lonely days, and all the new, scary stuff six-year-old me had to deal with. No friends, weird food, living in a Chicago apartment with cousins that first year, then our own apartment. And just when I'd made a few friends, moving again to Heron Lake. I don't know what I would have done if Mom hadn't brought Ruby and Cougar home from the Greyhound Rescue Center on my eighth birthday.

"What's your point?"

He shrugs. "I don't know." He stares down the hallway as if the answer is beyond these walls. "What if college isn't my thing?"

I laugh. He doesn't. And something in his expression unsettles me. "Of course it is. We've had this planned forever. You're just tired of school. You'll be fine."

His shoulders slump, too slight for anyone else to notice, and he avoids my eyes. "Yeah, I guess."

There's an uneasiness about him lately, more than usual. Maybe it's his parents – they've never been the warm-and-fuzzy types. Polite, always nice to me, but it ends there. I thought maybe it was an English thing, but now I know it's just a Channing thing. He probably misses Cat, now that she's tied up with getting her master's degree and hanging out with some new boyfriend.

"We're going to see the gym next. You'll like that." It's my third desperate attempt today to find something to grab his interest. "I heard they have great workout equipment."

He nods, showing zero enthusiasm despite his normal obsession with working out.

Maybe years of living in that house, with its aura of sadness and baby Jenna on the mantle, is starting to take a toll on Alec. As my friend wanders these halls, he looks ready to hit the road like Forrest Gump and never turn back. Maybe it's the secret he guards from the world. Whatever good Alec has done, whatever he's accomplished, is overshadowed by something he's never let me see. And without knowing why, I'm certain it has to do with the baby.

"Remember when you talked about becoming a gym teacher?" We head out of the science room and down another hall, where one wall is filled with quotes from famous authors. "That would be a good fit, right? You could coach soccer, too." I cringe inside, hearing my own words and realizing I sound like a parent trying to guide their kid. The worst part, though, is the note of desperation. No doubt he heard it, too.

"I guess. I don't know." He stares ahead, plodding along with the group, seemingly oblivious to the world around him.

"You should try one of the school counselors. They can help with figuring out majors." I pause to find the vaguest words possible for what I really want to say. "Other stuff, too." If only he'd talk to someone, maybe he'd find space to breath and freedom from whatever's crushing him.

His eyes narrow. "As in?"

And there it is: the defensiveness that creeps into his tone if there's even a hint of dealing with his issues. The reason for my futile attempt at carefully choosing my words.

"Whatever. I just know people talk to them about things sometimes. It might be helpful. Worth a try, right?"

The tour guide motions for the group to head left down another hallway and glances directly at Alec. He flashes a smile so fake I want to vomit, then turns back to me.

"No, it isn't. Not *everyone* needs help, Nathan. Not *everyone* has their entire life planned out like you do. I'm fine. You know who needs help? Your Ruby. Focus on *her*. She was limping in the yard."

We walk past more signs and he pauses when we reach a military banner with brochures about joining the various branches. American flags and stars fill in the spaces between the recruitment posters. Alec's eyes linger long enough for him to fall a few steps behind, but he's back at my side in seconds.

"What were you looking at?" Of all the stuff we've seen today, *that's* what catches his attention?

"I don't know. Posters and stuff."

"Yeah, *military* posters. Why would you be looking at military stuff?"

He stops. I do the same. People behind us sidestep to avoid walking into us.

"You keep wanting me to notice things, then when I do, you question it." A hint of anger laces Alec's words. "I'm just trying to figure things out, that'll all. Checking out options on the walls, seeing what's what. Do you *mind*?"

Wow, that escalated quickly. "No. Relax. I was just surprised. Look at whatever you want. I couldn't care less." I care a lot. We're coming here, to this school, in less than a year. There's no reason for him to be looking at options. This has been our plan forever. Go to the same school, ride there together, meet up for lunch if we can. I remind myself that Sean is going here, too, and our friend

Lola from down the block. A few others, as well. But Alec's the one I talk to about everything, the one who's been a constant in my life since leaving Peru. He can't possibly be thinking about something other than this school.

He starts walking again, and we catch up with the group. "We were talking about Ruby and her limp. What's the deal with that?"

We weren't. *He* was. But my counselor comment put him on edge, so we'll talk about Ruby.

"Don't know. Her eating's a little off, too. I'm taking her to the vet this afternoon. We have an appointment." And just like that, the conversation veers away from Alec. One of these days, I'm not going to let that happen. "It's probably no big deal. She'll be fine."

"I'm sorry, Nathan." Dr. Washington runs his finger along Ruby's leg X-rays as he peers through Coke bottle lenses. Ruby nudges him, comfortable with the man who's been her vet since she and Cougar joined our family. "Wish I had better news, but I suspect Ruby has bone cancer."

His words make no sense. She was limping. I figured she had a pebble in her foot, like last summer. Or a bee sting. Even a sprain; that's happened before, too. All easily treatable. I clutch the side of the exam table, dazed by the "C" word. Wondering how I hadn't noticed she'd lost six pounds. And waiting for him to say he made a mistake.

He doesn't.

"You can operate, right?"

"In some cases, yes, but this appears pretty advanced." He reaches into a cabinet, his hand emerging with a cookie-shaped treat. Ruby sniffs and gingerly takes it from his palm. "We'll have to run more tests to know for sure. Then we can talk about options."

My heart tries to convince my mind that "advanced"

means recovery will take a little longer. That's all. Because this is Ruby. Strong, courageous Ruby, who survived years of racing at a dog track before coming to live with us. *My* Ruby, who rescued eight-year-old me when I was alone in my room, friendless, missing my Chicago cousins, missing Peru, and hating Heron Lake. Until Alec came along, she and Cougar were my only friends. We'll beat this cancer. She'll be with me through high school and college. She'll be there to greet me when I come home from my shifts at the firehouse. She nudges me with her nose, just like she did back then, and I gently scratch between her ears.

"Are you okay?" The doctor's tone resonates the compassion of someone who's painfully experienced in delivering bad news.

My throat thickens and I keep my eyes on Ruby, knowing I'll lose it if I see the sympathy on his face. I run my hand along her back, feeling her weight loss and hating myself for not paying closer attention.

"Yeah."

"You've got a sweetheart here, Nathan. It's plain to see you love her. But when the time comes, the time comes. Know what I mean?" Dr. Washington reads a chart on his computer screen, then turns back toward me. "Holdin' on won't do either of you any good."

I nod, unable to do anything more. He shouldn't be using phrases like "when the time comes." That time is a long, long ways off. Years from now. He's always been great with the dogs, but he should know better.

"I've seen my share of pups that endured a lot of pain because their owners loved them too much to let go. But real love, well, sometimes that means doin' the hard thing."

"Okay." I get it, I do. But that's far off in the future. No need to dwell on it now.

He explains he's going to do a needle aspirate to get cells from the tumor and will draw a vial of blood as well.

When he finishes, he tells Ruby she's a "good dog" and says he'll call with the test results. She looks at me, those sweet eyes saying "Let's go home," and we head outside to a different world than the one we woke up to this morning.

"You'll be fine, girl." I pat her neck. "Don't you worry, you'll be fine."

Chapter 6

Nathan
Thursday, Midnight

We ride past houses on the dark, sleepy streets, our bikes providing the silent escape we needed. Cutting across the lake would have been quicker, but our aluminum canoe has been resting peacefully in the shed's hospital wing since Alec and I dropped it last summer. His fault, of course, but he blames it on me. Above us, stars flicker in a sea of unending blackness and a ghostly haze outlines the moon. Like a warning. Adrenaline and fear pump through my veins. Cicadas croon from their hideaways in the branches above. No music, traffic, or barking dogs. No talking. It's not bad. Sort of peaceful, actually.

"Kind of cool, riding around this late." Alec's voice kills the tranquility.

"Yeah."

"It's like that summer we first met. Remember the backyard sleepover?"

I nod, knowing he's trying to lighten things up. "What a disaster. First it takes an hour to set up your dad's old military tent, then Kingman spots our flashlights and calls the cops." I don't mention the spider incident, my first encounter with Alec's arachnophobia. One Daddy

Longlegs on the outside of the tent and it took me ten minutes to calm him down and another ten to convince him to stay outside. That part never comes up when we reminisce about that night.

Alec laughs. "Yeah, I don't think they were too happy with Kingman that night. Man, that guy must have a telescope by every window."

"Yep, and I get to hear all his gossip." The old guy decided I was his best friend the day Mom sent me over with a plate of paella. "Can't believe it's been ten summers since we moved here."

I thought I would die when my parents said we were leaving the city and moving to a house in the suburbs. My best friend and cousins waved goodbye from the curb while I sat in the back seat, watching my whole world disappear. Less than two hours later, we arrived in Heron Lake Village. I hated everything about it...except the lake. Fishing in summer, hockey in winter, and a place to be alone at night.

Alec's head nods in the darkness. "Went fast. I can still picture it, though. You know, that first day. You out there trying to fish. Doing it all wrong."

I roll my eyes at the phrase he uses *every* time we talk about that hot, sticky July day. There was nothing wrong with the way I was fishing. My bobber floated a few feet offshore as I sat comfortably in the shade of a weeping willow, enjoying the peace and quiet after living on a noisy Chicago street. Until Alec sauntered by.

"Blimey, that cast was pure rubbish. How do you expect to catch any bloody fish?"

I hated him instantly. "Speak English."

"*You* speak English."

And so it began. Somehow that led to graphic novels and skateboarding and girls. By the time school started, we were best friends.

The memory fades as we turn our bikes onto Aspen Drive and I point toward the far end of the block. "Almost there."

"Okay, now what? I don't suppose you've thought of a plan."

His comment grates me, mostly because he's right. With an aggravated sigh I answer, "Of course I did."

Darkness prevents me from seeing his eye-roll, but it happened. No doubt.

We slow down in unison, realizing we need to come up with something quick. I survey the area, easier now that my night vision has kicked in. Here and there, leaves flutter through the darkness like falling shadows. A ghostly white tomcat trots out from the yard next to Haylie's, stops to assess us, then slinks off in the opposite direction.

We need to ditch the bikes if we're going to nose around her house. I want to see the backyard, too, and the alley behind it. Maybe there's a piece of evidence left undetected by the cops and feds—a frantically scrawled note with a name or address. Anything. I can just imagine presenting my key piece of evidence to Agent Alessio, who would let me tag along in appreciation for my mind-blowing detective skills. We'd bust through the kidnapper's door and Haylie would rush into the arms of her hero.

"Look." I point past Haylie's house to a particularly dark area. "Her house is right near the path that leads to the grade school."

The first section of the path is bordered by a low fence, the kind with wooden beams that cowboys sit on in those western movies. It's located in an area beyond the streetlight's illumination. Perfect cover for our bikes. We lean them against the fence posts, walking silent as that tomcat toward Haylie's backyard. When I stop, Alec bumps into me. My gasp reverberates through the town. At least, it sounds that way to me. I freeze, expecting every porch light to flicker on, but the houses remain dark.

"Maybe we should split up," I say.

"No way," Alec whispers through gritted teeth. No shadow of his carefree smile is visible.

I keep moving forward, afraid if I stop he might change his mind. "But there might be cops around. If we split up and one of us gets caught, then maybe the other could get away."

He stops. There's no choice but to do the same. "No deal. I'm doing this for you, but that doesn't mean I have to do it your way." Threads of fear weave through every word. "We stick together, or I'm gone."

"Okay, fine," I whisper. "We stick together. Let's just look around the yard and garage."

We near the gate. The backdoor squeaks open, followed by a click. Alec grabs my arm, then lets go, probably hoping I didn't notice. Cloaked by a tall, gangly bush, we flatten against the side of the house. Thorns scrape my arm and graze my cheek, but I stifle my "ouches," wishing we'd landed in a less painful spot. My breaths come slow and shallow as I strain to listen. In the backyard, a man talks quietly on a phone. I turn toward Alec.

"I can't hear anything. I have to get closer."

My quivering whisper reaches Alec, who shakes his head and leans within an inch of my face. "Are you daft?"

"I have to hear what he's saying. Need to see who it is. That's why we're here."

Alec shakes his head again, more vigorously this time.

"You stay here," I say. "I'll be right back." I don't wait for his predictable response. As I move toward the yard, he calls me an indistinguishable name. Pretty sure it isn't "mate."

Sliding between the house's outside wall and the prickly bush wreaks havoc on my bare arms. A thorn hooks my T-shirt and hangs on tight. I finally detach myself with a hard tug and continue to the back corner of the house, while my booming heart is probably announcing my presence to the mystery man. The bush ends. I proceed, glad to be out of the thorns, but feeling vulnerable out in the open. Slow footsteps lumber across the wooden deck in my direction. Self-preservation tells me to run back to the protective cover of the bush, but I need to hear his words. Hopefully, the darkness is cover enough.

"I'm surprised she's not sleeping." The mystery man pauses to listen. "How do I know what the motions mean? I'm not there. Maybe she's hungry or confused. Maybe even scared. Could be anything."

A cricket chirps in the distance, its solo the only sound breaking the silence while I wait for the voice to speak again. *Who's* not sleeping? Haylie? He said "motions." That has to refer to her signing. Horrific images assault my brain. Haylie caged or locked in a basement. Haylie bruised and bloody. Alone and terrified. Stuffed in a trunk and getting farther away by the minute. Resolve tightens my jaw as I stand just steps away from evil.

Everything in me wants to pummel him, but I wait, knowing his next words might reveal her location. If he doesn't say something soon, I'll go insane. My fingers clench into sweaty palms. In my entire life, I never imagined killing anything, let alone a person. But if he hurts her...

The scumbag sighs. "You have to keep in mind she's still fairly young, and the people she trusts and loves aren't around. Just take care of her while I'm away. Is that too much to ask? Hopefully..." His voice cracks. He clears his throat while I hold my breath, awaiting his next words. "Hopefully, I'll be there soon, but right now only one thing matters."

That's it. I can't take it anymore. I *have* to see who's talking. Muscles tensed and ready to fight, I peek around the corner. A small backdoor light illuminates part of the yard, along with his profile. There's something familiar. Black skin. Glasses. Short cropped beard. I step forward for a better look and my foot brushes a small round bush. A furry white demon leaps out, screeches like the undead, and races across the yard in a blur. I jump and yell. Alec curses loud enough to wake people in the next town, and we sprint toward our bikes even faster than the cat.

But not before I see Russell Summers' face.

Those Tour de France racers got nothin' on us. We fly through deserted streets, Alec behind me shouting "Leg it, Nathan, leg it!" I'm tempted to toss back a "Speak English!" but now's not the time. About a mile from home, we slow down. Alec glides up next to me. One glance at each other and we bust out laughing—releasing a truckload of anxiety and fear. Like mindless drunks, we go at it until we can hardly breathe.

"You idiot." Alec controls his laughter just enough to talk. "What did you yell for?"

"That cat scared the crap out of me. Jumped outta the bush. What did *you* yell for?"

"Because *you* scared *me!*"

"Oh, man." I stop to catch my breath, and Mr. Summers' face flashes back into my brain with a sobering effect. "Alec, I saw him. Haylie's stepdad."

I expect a dramatic gasp or one of his crazy English slang words, but Alec simply shrugs. "So what? He lives there. It doesn't prove he's the guy. Maybe he couldn't sleep. I mean, his daughter's gone missing."

A dog barks in someone's backyard, followed by the sound of a door opening and closing. Dying leaves rustle in the breeze, then stop. The street is swallowed by an eerie silence.

I lean toward Alec, afraid someone might hear. "I heard him. He knows where she is. He's in on it!"

This time his brows arch. "No way."

"Seriously." I relay the conversation, word for word.

"Brilliant! You got him!" He congratulates me with a punch to the arm.

I push down on my pedal and take off, Alec on my tail.

"Come on, I have to go tell the agents."

We head back at a less frantic pace, but half a mile from home Alec's front tire crunches over a piece of broken glass. The gash is big enough to deflate the tire in seconds, leaving us no choice but to hoof it...and there goes our game plan. Alec checks the time on his phone as we round the corner of our block, where a car is parked in front of my house. Black. Unfamiliar. This can't be good. The yellow glow of Kingman's old-fashioned streetlamp reveals two dark shapes in the front seat. They must be watching through the rear view, because by the time we notice them, they're stepping out. Both wear suits, but one stands out. Tall and thirtyish, with a familiar smirk on his pasty face.

"It's Smirley," I whisper to Alec. "Remember, the one I didn't like?"

"Judging from his expression, he doesn't fancy you much either."

We creep toward him, knowing it would look bad to stop, but certainly not anxious to reach our destination.

"Evening, gentlemen." Hands in pockets, he struts in our direction. "I assume you're familiar with the curfew laws in this town."

He's thoroughly enjoying the moment. I look at Alec, wishing I could beam him back to the safety of his living room.

"Yes, sir." I respond for both of us.

"Do you often go bike riding at this hour?" He looks directly at me. It's a stupid question, but he awaits the obvious answer.

"No, sir."

"You're pretty scratched up there, buddy." He looks at my arms. "And is that a fresh tear in your shirt?"

Buddy. His mocking tone makes my skin crawl. Alec stands there, silently holding on to his bike. *Let him go home, Smirley. Leave him alone.* I look at my arms and shirt, incapable of providing any justification for my appearance. He may as well just hang a noose from the highest tree.

"Looks like your friend's sporting a few scratches as well," the other guy says. He is dark-skinned, with short curly hair and the hint of an island accent. Maybe Jamaican, but it's just a guess. I glance around, hoping to see Agent Alessio, but she's nowhere in sight.

"I find this interesting." Smirley rubs his chin between his thumb and index finger, Sherlock Holmes style. It's almost funny. Emphasis on the *almost*. "I have a missing girl, and one of our suspects sneaks out of the house at midnight and comes home all scratched up. Now if you were an FBI agent, Nate, what conclusion would you come to?"

I look down. He's talking to me like I'm a child, and it's making me nuts. My eyes rise, locking on his. "If I were an FBI agent, I'd know better than to jump to conclusions. If I were an FBI agent, I'd know things aren't always what they seem."

One side of my brain shouts "Stop, Nathan. This won't end well," but the other half has no intention of stopping before its point is made.

"If I were an FBI agent and there was a girl missing, I'd be out looking for her." That's it. I mentally brace myself for the wrecking ball to hit.

"And that's just what I was doing, *Nate*, until I got a call from my partner saying your parents reported you missing. She would have come herself, you see, but unfortunately, she's tied up at the Summers' house where, coincidentally, there was a disturbance just a short time ago. When they checked the perimeter of the house, they found a tiny piece of blue cloth, like the color of your T-shirt there, clinging to a bush."

No more wondering why my favorite agent isn't here.

"So, on the one hand, I know you weren't with Haylie, but on the other, I know something's up, and I'm extremely curious as to what that something might be.

Get my drift?"

"Yeah." It is the best I can do, given the circumstances. I maintain eye contact, even though I want to look anywhere but at him.

Smirley leans back against the car, folding his arms, like some Men in Black clone. All he's missing is the shades. "And right about the time I finished talking with your parents, I got a call saying you two were spotted heading this way."

Alec and I look at each other. Spotted? There wasn't a soul on the streets. What do these guys do, hide in trees? We're caught off guard, and he loves it.

"We're a pretty sneaky bunch, Nate. That's how we catch bad guys."

Somehow, he knows I hate being called Nate. I don't know how, but he knows. Just like he knows I'm in no position to voice my feelings on the matter. Because it boils down to this: Smirley's right. Haylie's missing, someone was creeping around her house, and here I am after midnight, covered in scratches. So it's Smirley, three; Nathan, zero. The name thing is insignificant and not worth digging myself a deeper grave when this one is already closing in around me.

"As for you, Alec..."

I can practically feel the throbbing of Alec's pulse.

"What do you have to say? Were you involved in anything you care to share with us?"

"No sir." Alec's voice cracks on the "sir."

"Alec has nothing to do with this, Agent Smirley." I'm respectful now. Even friendly. Ready to be "buddies." Whatever it takes for him to leave Alec out of it. "How about if Alec goes home and I'll tell you all about what just happened?"

"Oh, believe me, we're *all* going to talk about what just happened. But for the moment, Alec here can go back home with Agent Davies. His parents are anxious to talk to him."

In the dim porch light, all the color drains from Alec's face. Mr. Channing used to be in the British SAS, a Special Forces military unit. Kind of like the Navy Seals, I guess. And now he's a baker. Go figure. But that whole military thing is still inside him. He's got this neck vein that bulges and pulsates whenever he's going ballistic. It will be clearly visible tonight.

Alec stares at his bike handles. Maybe he prefers the company of Smirley and Davies over what awaits at home.

"Well you better get a move on." Smirley's rattlesnake eyes glimmer like he's just swallowed a mouse and is savoring the taste. "We want to get this over with in time for your father to start the dough for his famous chocolate-hazelnut biscuits. And try not to wake your sister. She has a big test in the morning."

He knows about the beautiful Cat. He knows about the bakery and the British word for cookies. He knows way too much about our lives for someone who's just been in the picture since this morning. My stomach churns again, like when Agent Alessio looked through my emails. These people have violated my world, stolen personal, intangible pieces of my life.

Alec turns toward home, still fixated on the bike handles. I never should have asked him to come with me, but regret is useless. There's no fixing it now. No way to stop his parents from making him more miserable than he is at this moment. I just hope I don't lose my best friend on top of everything else. I'm already losing my mind over what's happening to Haylie. Someone needs to find her. Every minute counts. Instead of questioning us, these guys should be searching every corner of the planet, every basement and alley and abandoned building.

Smirley nods toward the house and I head for the front door, wondering how a day that started out so normal could end in such gut-wrenching disaster.

Chapter 7

Haylie
Friday Morning

My brain analyzes the video message for the thousandth time since recording it last night. It can't be money. There's another reason; I'm sure of it. They want something from Mom or Dad, but what? If it's Mom, it's got to be connected to her work as a physicist for ZetaLab. She said it's one of the top labs in the country. Over the years, she's always used phrases like "quantum physics" and "particle research," so there's got to be information or discoveries that bad guys might want. But she's also a board member of a group trying to abolish human trafficking. Could be that, too. On the other hand, if they're targeting *Dad*, they want something related to his work at Wild Things. That's crazy, though. What could they want from an animal rescue place? Whatever they're after, if they don't get it soon, my future looks short...and excruciatingly painful.

Slowly. I try to erase the word from my mind, but it keeps reappearing. How can such a bland word become an instrument of suffering? *Slowly.* Images of agonizing torture pour into my head. Bloody scenes from movies. Gruesome accounts from history books. It is unfathomable what humans can do to each other, what horrifically creative ways they devise to torture and kill. And it's unfortunate that normal people like me, who aren't murderous psychos, can graphically imagine all of those vile scenarios. As if being stuck in this chair isn't enough. And the worst part is, I don't know if they have my family, or what they might be doing to *them* to get whatever it is they want. It astounds me that our little garden-variety family could be the target of people gripped by the demons of greed or power or whatever ugly desires "justify" crushing others to get what they want. Are they cruel enough to take an eight-year-old? To hurt him? If I let myself think about Ben, there will be nothing left of me.

The only force that keeps me from utterly imploding is faith. It gives me hope. Strength. Reminds me that I'm not alone. That there's someone bigger than my fears and doubts and weaknesses. And if my life ends in this shabby motel before I even get to wear my first prom dress or go on college tours, at least there's a way better place waiting for me. But I can't help dreading the moments just before that happens, or knowing the devastating impact it will have on my family.

A hand grazes the back of my head. I jerk. Gasp. My pulse races...yet again. My focus on figuring out their motives kept me from noticing the vibrations of someone approaching. My blindfold drops and Jeans steps in front of me, still masked. He unties me, grabs his gun, and hands me the same note they give me each time. *Don't scream! Bathroom break and 10 minutes to stretch and drink.*

Fear triggered by the gun is quickly replaced by a wave of joy. It's the kind of joy I used to get from Imani signing to me, or walking through the Amazon, or celebrating with Mom when her group succeeds in rescuing girls. In forty-eight hours, everything has changed. This is my new reality: a few minutes of movement are now the highlight of my existence. I stand, stretching muscles that have sat far too long. Muscles that long to run down the lake path, feeling alive and free. Every minute is precious, because unlike Grizzly, this guy sticks to the schedule, timing me on his phone stopwatch. Never mind that another minute or two wouldn't impact his life in any way, while it would mean the world to me.

Each time the blindfold comes off, I scan the room and my captor, hoarding ridiculous details like precious gems. Green tic-tacs on the counter, black backpack with red stitching on the floor, navy blue running shoes next to the door. Jeans always wears a brown leather wristband with a cobra etched into it. Maybe that means something. He's thinner than the others. Seems younger, even with his face covered. I gather little bits at a time, careful not to stare at anything so he doesn't suspect I'm storing away the information.

Just before my ten minutes of "freedom" ends, I glance at Jeans and notice something I hadn't seen before. With the glow from the floor lamp hitting his ski-masked face, I can see his eyes. His very green eyes. One more thing for my files. He notices me looking at him and walks toward me with that gun pointed straight at my chest, then points to the chair. My heart sinks, wanting to go anywhere but that dreaded chair, but the gun is powerful motivation. I sit and he tosses the blindfold and plastic ties onto my lap. It's our routine. I secure my ankles and put on the blindfold, then he binds my wrists to the arms of the chair and double checks everything. He's made it clear that any attempt to fight ends with me dead, or at the very least, losing a limb.

I've returned to darkness, left only with my thoughts and prayers. They can't take those away. But my heart sinks as I remember they do, in fact, steal those away every time they drug me. I'm not drugged now, though, and there's nothing to do but think.

Mom's ZetaLab job is a good place to start, so I zero in

on some of the sciency stuff she's told me about the huge project she's working on. Secrecy. Radioactive waste. Something about converting it to something else. I search for what that "something else" might be and come up blank, wishing I had paid closer attention. All I remember is her complaining about problems with the formula, but that could either be math or chemical. She resented how it cut into her family time because she often had to stay late at the lab or bring work home. But despite the resentment, it became an obsession. Must be a very, very big deal. Lately, I've noticed her taking melatonin to sleep at night, and aspirin for headaches. So there's that.

I move on to Mom's involvement with Abolish Slavery Now. If my captors are part of a human trafficking ring, maybe Mom's group messed up something for them. My memory traipses back a few weeks to her celebrating because ASN rescued a group of five Cambodian girls forced into prostitution. They'd been promised jobs as nannies in the United States, but it was all a scam. Testimony from the girls led to the capture of two of the traffickers, but a couple more are still at large. They could be my kidnappers. This whole thing could be retaliation for that rescue. Ransoming me could be a way for them to get their girls back or send a message for ASN to back off. Definitely plausible.

But so is the Wild Things theory. Switching gears again, I picture that horrid day when a small group of college kids entered the rescue center's grounds. They carried signs and said they were animal rights activists, but that didn't make sense. All the animal rights groups support what we're doing at Wild Things.

"We don't breed, train, or cage our animals," Dad told them. "We don't make them pose with people for photos. They're not our toys or pets. Each one has been rescued from a terrible situation."

But this weird group didn't seem to get it. With scrunched-up faces and their mouths flapping open and shut repeatedly, they held their signs up high. A girl in a tie-dyed sweatshirt carried a poster that read, "Send Imani Home to Cameroon!" I remember thinking she must be crazy. Imani couldn't survive in the forest anymore. The other lowland gorillas wouldn't accept her now. She'd be all alone, without a troop, aching for the family she loved and trusted, and wondering why "Girl" wasn't there to give her hugs and strawberry-banana smoothies.

My mind scans the image of that crowd for potential kidnapping suspects and lands on the shaggy, blond guy jabbing at the sky with his "Free Them All!" sign. His mouth moved like a bullet train as he yelled. I caught a few words as they flew out: *captive, inhumane, back to the forest*, punctuated by stomping the ground with his pricy new hiking boots. No way those things ever touched the soft, earthy, decomposing floor of the rain forest. No way those livid blue eyes were ever awed by a thousand shades of green, or the small splotches of sunlight fighting their way through the treetop canopy. None of them knew a thing about what happens when a baby gorilla is separated from her mother. Her tribe. They had fancy shoes and anger, but not a clue.

Vibrations on the floor jar me from the memory but quickly end. I keep telling myself he's not going to hurt me. He would have done it by now. The aroma of chocolate drifts my way. Not just chocolate, though. Something else. Peanut butter. Grizzly always offers me something when he eats, but not this guy. The sweet aroma of my favorite candy swirls around me 'til I can almost taste it. If only the absence of peanut butter cups was my biggest problem.

Focus, Haylie. The protesters. I picture Dad trying to reason with them, explaining that we don't promote wildlife in captivity, we just try to save those who have been neglected and abused. But they just kept chanting "Set Imani free! Set Imani free!" And with their perfect ears, they never listened.

I shake my head, remembering that poor little thing. Just a baby. Half dead, starving, and dehydrated when the rangers found her. Where were those protesters when we were nursing her back to health? By the time they came tromping into Wild Things, she'd been with us for three years.

Maybe this is some twisted form of justice, putting me in captivity just like Imani. Or they're planning to trade me for Imani's freedom. The worst part is, Dad will do it. He'll give in to the crazies just to get me back. But she'll die for sure in the hands of those well-intentioned idiots.

It's the theory that makes the most sense. Except it doesn't. Grizzly, Suit, and Jeans don't fit the profile. Those demonstrators weren't much older than me. But if it wasn't the protesters, and it's not rape or human trafficking, *thank God,* and we don't have the kind of money worth kidnapping for...I'm back to square one. Maybe square two, because recognizing that patch of white in Grizzly's beard unsettles me enough to wonder if my captivity is connected to that vague memory.

And then there's Nathan.

Need to talk. Can you meet me in 10 behind your garage?

The text keeps creeping back into my head. Logic tells me that message is absolute proof Nathan is involved. Thinking otherwise would be so naïve. I know better than to let my heart call the shots. There's no point in picturing his shy smile and dark cocoa eyes or imagining us having pizza. Talking and laughing. Clearly, he's tied into the kidnapping, so there shouldn't be one second of me wondering what it would feel like for those strong swimmer's arms to wrap around me, with the warmth of his body against mine. His lips touching my lips.

Unless...and everything but my brain is leaning this way...I should trust the completely illogical instincts telling me he's got nothing to do with it.

Chapter 8

Nathan
Friday Morning

My blaring alarm opens my eyes to morning light and the memory of staring at the clock until 3:30 a.m., but in this bleary moment, I can't remember why. I kill the noise and sink back into my oversized pillow. Five more minutes. That's all I need. My foggy brain is just lucid enough to remember it's Friday. That Language Arts paper is due. A quiz in Physics. Not feeling rock solid about that, but Haylie will probably get another A.

Haylie.

I ache to escape back into those few hours of sleep, but it's too late. Reality smacks me in the head like Alec's soccer ball. Haylie's missing. The FBI. The night ride with Alec. Smirley waiting by the house.

In the kitchen, I pour a glass of grape juice and toss bread into the toaster. Cougar stops crunching his breakfast long enough to turn and look at me.

"Yes, it's me." I pat his shoulder. "Just like *every* morning."

Ruby's already back in her dog bed, her bowl still half full of food that Cougar will likely devour. She raises her head a few inches off the cushion to greet me with a soft whine. My knees hit the carpet next to her and I feed her another peanut-butter coated pill. "How's my girl?" She rests her head back on her cushion and looks up at me. Pain veils her eyes. "Be strong, girl. I can't lose you." I close my eyes and try to push away the hard, cold fact that a brutal disease is ravaging her body, and I can't do anything to stop it.

"She needs to leave us, Nathan." Mom speaks softly, her words laced with compassion. She loves Ruby, too. We all do. "You know this, *verdad*? You must do what's right for her."

My heart cringes at the thought. Everything is changing. High school is ending. Alec is acting weird with his Saturday afternoon disappearing act. And Haylie. Oh man, Haylie.

I can't let Ruby go. She's family. *My* family.

"But this morning we have other things to discuss." Mom scrambles a gooey mixture of eggs, milk and cheese in the mini frying pan. Heavy eyelids tell me she didn't sleep much either. Her face is pale and tight, with no trace of her usual morning smile. No cheery *"buenos días"* offered up to start my morning. She is not happy with me because I did something *"estúpido* and dangerous and irresponsible."

"Do not scare me again the way you did last night. Is this clear?"

I nod, having nothing to contribute.

"You are my world, *mijo*." She sprinkles salt into the pan. "Last night, my world got very dark. And that young agent, I do not like him. Did you tell him everything so he will not come back?" She sets my bowl of eggs on the table, but not before scooping some onto a paper plate for Ruby.

"Yes, yes, everything." It was supposed to be Agent Alessio, not Smirley, hearing my story of Russel Summers' phone conversation and what I'd found out about him on the Internet. Smirley made it clear he was not impressed.

"Oh, so you did a little detective work, eh?" His look told me they'd done it about forty hours ago. He was baiting me, and though the lure was tempting, my mouth stayed shut. Clenched, but shut.

"Sooo, would that be the death row Russell Summers in Texas who murdered his grandfather, the drug dealer Russell Summers out of California, or my personal favorite, the Canadian Russell Summers who gets arrested for climbing skyscrapers?" Smirley makes zero effort to conceal his irritation with this midnight call out. "I'm sorry, I almost forgot the Florida Russell Summers who kidnapped his neighbor's Chihuahua."

I had just glanced at the headlines and was in too much of a hurry to actually read the articles. Big mistake. A heat wave swept my face.

"And by the way, three of those Russells are white, so…"

Standing guard next to my chair, Cougar had pointed his long, skinny muzzle in my direction and licked my hand. He might not be the toughest creature in Heron Lake, but he was there for me. Ruby sat obediently next to Mom, but her big brown eyes had lost their sweetness, hardening to coal as she glared at Smirley. My buddies. And to think I was so disappointed when Mom didn't bring home a German Shepherd.

I grab the bowl, glad last night is over, and head to the living room to watch the morning news. A weird habit, according to my friends, but music videos and cartoons don't cut it for me in the morning. I need to know what's going on in my part of the world before heading into it. Especially when my almost-girlfriend has been kidnapped.

"Good morning, Chicago." News Anchor Miya Turner flaunts dazzling teeth that would make her dentist proud.

I plop onto the couch, anxiously awaiting word that Haylie's okay, she's been rescued, she's home with her family, eating Cheerios and choosing an outfit for school.

The smile fades as sunny Miya readies her expression for the top story. "Seventeen-year-old Haylie Summers is still missing from her Heron Lake Village home, where she disappeared Wednesday night. Police believe Miss Summers, a deaf student at Beethoven High School, was forcibly taken sometime between seven and seven-thirty p.m." Haylie smiles at me from the TV screen, wearing that purple sweater she wore the day I asked her out.

The reporter's recap does little more than mirror everything I already know. Haylie's been kidnapped and nobody knows why or by who or even if she's still alive. I see Agent Alessio's eyes flash with determination as she utters sound bites to the media and asks "anyone with any knowledge to please contact the Heron Lake police or FBI." Just like that, it's over, and we're on to a factory fire in one of the western suburbs. Black smoke billows from broken windows, firemen with gritty faces work together in a battle of man against the elements. I watch and eat the eggs because Mom made them for me, but they have to squeeze past my tightening throat before landing in my crunched-up stomach.

"Hurry, Nathan." Mom calls from the kitchen. "It is getting late."

I grab my backpack and head to the corner with my favorite Tiny Kingdoms song resonating through my earbuds. Passing my neighbor's house, I'm careful to stay on the pavement. If I bend a blade of his precious grass, I'll be sentenced to a discussion on respecting other people's property. Lately, though, Mr. Kingman's attention has been centered on sweet old Mrs. Vitalli, whose little dog traipses across his beloved lawn whenever she takes a walk. To Kingman's dismay, this happens daily. To my greater dismay, I have to hear about it.

A voice breaks through my music that is definitely not coming from any member of the band.

"How ya doin' there, Nathan?"

I can't do this today. Really. "Okay, Mr. Kingman. You?"

"She did it again yesterday. Right on schedule. 9 a.m." As expected, he doesn't bother to answer the question. There are far more critical issues at hand. "Came walkin' on by with that little poodle or what's-it-called and let it walk right on my grass, even the new grass that's just startin' to grow!" He ambles down the stairs and meets me on the sidewalk.

Someone just shoot me. Please. "Lily's a cocker spaniel, Mr. K. Poodles have that curly fur. Anyway, she probably didn't hurt your grass. She's pretty light."

"Well, now, that's not the point."

Of course it's not. The point, which he is missing entirely, is that he needs to get a life. A real one, with purpose and friends and something other than whatever *this* is. I pull my ear bud out and let it dangle over my shoulder. "She's a real nice lady, you know." My teeth clench in an attempt to imprison the volume that's aching to escape. "She probably doesn't even know it bothers you."

"Now you sound just like my nephew with the crazy ponytail. He came by with sammiches I like from that place down the street from where he'll be workin' in a couple weeks." Mr. Kingman bends for a closer look at the grass, keeping one hand pressed against his back. "He likes to get a look-see at his construction sites before his next job begins. Lucky for me, it was right by that sammich place. Pulled pork with coleslaw on top. Now *that's* a sammich."

And here we go.

"Yep, they're finally gonna do somethin' with that abandoned hotel. 'Bout time, I say. It's been sittin' empty for years. He says it's gonna be real nice when they're all done. Anyways, he talks just like you. Thinks she's not doin' it on purpose." He points to the grass. "Look trampled to you?"

Alec would love this. More ammunition for harassing me about being Kingman's "best mate." Squatting down, I pretend to examine the grass. "Nope. No harm done."

"Hmph." He squints at the patch of grass, trying to find a damaged blade that I missed. So you say she's nice?"

"Yeah, real nice. Sorry, I need to get going." I take a step, but Mr. Kingman shakes his head as though we're in the midst of a political debate.

"No, no. You're fine." He checks his watch. "It'll be five minutes yet."

He knows the school bus schedule. Not creepy at all.

"I wonder where she goes every mornin'," he continues. "You think she goes someplace special, or just walks?"

"Really don't know, Mr. K." I look around, hoping for some urgent matter to call me away from this ridiculous conversation. Leaves rustle, ducks waddle across the street, but nothing saves me from my geriatric neighbor.

He stares at Mrs. Vitalli's house. "Seems to walk with a purpose, you know? Maybe she meets another gal for coffee. There's that fancy coffee place just a few blocks from here." He points in the general direction of Java Joe's. "Four buckaroos for a cup of coffee. Now that's just crazy, if you ask me."

"Again, wouldn't know." Where's a school bus when you need one? Niceness is a curse. The poor guy is just lonely, basically an okay neighbor, but still...why me? Why can't he have these conversations with Alec? The answer is obvious. Because he's not a hot girl. It's just the way life goes. Alec gets the girls, I get the lonely old man. "Could be, but speaking of going someplace, I kinda have to go or I'll miss my bus."

"Oh yeah, yeah, you go on to school now. School's important, you know. I better get to waterin', anyhow. That seedling grass has to get watered every day. I remember one time I planted some grass seed and then I got sick for a few days..."

Oh no, you don't. "See ya, Mr. K." I wave and turn. It's the only way.

"All right, you get going now," he shouts to my back. "I'll probably be out when you get back."

I make a mental note to take the long way home.

Three minutes to go before the bus arrives and the whole school routine begins, but there is nothing routine about this day. There's no way I'll be concentrating on trig, Shakespeare, rain forest destruction and thermodynamics. Not today. Not 'til she's home safe. I head to the corner, where Alec arrives a minute later.

"Hey." I turn off my music. There's so much to talk about.

"Hey, yourself." His words bear an unfamiliar monotone. The woodsy scent of his cologne tells me he hit that store at the mall again. Probably last Saturday during his weekly disappearing act. Few things besides cologne and girls come between Alec Channing and his money. I don't know if the girls get drawn in by the cologne or the accent or his endless flirting. Whatever he's got...they like it. A couple of guys, too, but Alec's all about the girls.

"How did it go?"

Alec sets his backpack on the sidewalk. "Just perfect. We all had a wicked good time talking to Smirley's sidekick. Dad particularly enjoyed the conversation, especially since he'd been up before dawn." Alec's eyes lock on mine. "School will actually be the highlight of my day, thanks to you. I just got saddled with more hours at the bakery, without pay. So that's how it went."

"Look, Alec. I'm really sorry. Never meant for you..."

"Save it."

The bus arrives and, as always, I seek out two empty seats and sit down. Alec keeps going, though, sitting two rows behind me. Wow. He hasn't pulled that since I told one of his girlfriends that he's deathly afraid of spiders. And once before, when I asked a second time about his baby sister and he said, "She's dead! What more do you need to know?" He didn't talk to me for two days.

I plop my backpack on the seat next to me,

unaccustomed to the extra space, and stare out a window that hasn't been washed since...ever. Maybe he'll be okay by lunch. Until then, there's got to be something I can do, someone I can talk to. *Some* way to get information that will lead me to Haylie. The bus lumbers past houses, a strip mall, my favorite taco place, and more houses before stopping in the bus lane at school. I pause, wondering if I should wait for Alec, then move forward with the rest of the herd, deciding to give him some space.

Kimiko is opening her locker as I come up behind her. She and Haylie always talk there before first period. Her normally spiky, black hair is flat today, her ebony eyes outlined in the pale pink created by tears. Our school's volleyball superstar looks like she wouldn't have the energy for a serve. Must've had a long night, just like me. I stand in front of her, waiting for her to see me, but she seems oblivious to all the activity around her. She looks up, gasps and jumps back.

I'm sorry, I sign. *I'm sorry I scared you.*

It's okay.

Do you know about Haylie? Do you know information? Man, I'm horrible at this. Hopefully, she gets it. One wrong bend of the fingers and who knows what I might be saying.

She shakes her head no. *They asked me about you,* she signs.

Creepy to think the FBI is asking people what they think of me. What if they ask Bella? She hasn't talked to me since our disastrous first and only date at Café Luis. Man, that girl never stops talking. With my luck they'll question Miguel, the only guy on the swim team who's hated me ever since I started beating his times. This could really get ugly. Uglier than it is already.

They asked me many questions, too. I keep it simple so I don't mess up. *Do you know Haylie's father?* Really wish I had looked up the sign for "stepfather" last night.

Yes. He is very nice. He works at Wild Things Rescue Center. He is the head …

The last word eludes me. She's going too fast for me and using signs I don't know. Important words. Desperation battles embarrassment and wins. I look at her with a confused expression. *What?*

She spells it out, then sees my face and repeats it slower. I nod, finally getting that he's a veterinarian.

He lets us feed the animals. He and Haylie have been teaching Imani sign language. She spells Imani, but I have no idea who she's talking about. She sighs, pulls out her cell and hands it to me with the contact screen open. Why didn't *I* think of that? We exchange numbers.

Imani is a young gorilla they rescued after poachers killed her mother in Camaroon. It was even in the newspaper.

You think Mr. Summers could be involved in the kidnapping?

She shakes her head. *No way. He loves her like his own child. He's been Haylie's father since she was seven.*

He may have fooled *her*, but I'm not buying it. I heard what he said last night. He *had* to be talking about Haylie.

She glances at the hallway clock and grimaces. *We have to go.*

Wait. What does her mom do?

She's a physicist for ZetaLab. Super smart. Very nice.

ZetaLab. I know that place. Impressive. *Thanks. I'll tell you if I hear anything. Will you do the same?*

Yes. She nods just as the bell rings, and we take off in opposite directions.

Not what I expected, but interesting. At least now I know something more. With seconds left before Language Arts, I race off to class with my backpack flopping against my shoulder. Mrs. Barnes looks up as I enter the classroom.

"Ah, Mr. Boliva. Nice of you to join us. Please take a seat. We are continuing yesterday's discussion of *Hamlet*.

Perhaps you could explain why some people thought Hamlet was acting crazy?"

A hundred percent of my brain is wrapped around a real, here-and-now, life-and-death situation, and she wants me to talk about *Hamlet*. I blurt out the first thought that flies into my brain, with zero time between thinking and vocalizing. "Maybe because he knows things that other people don't know. Someone he loves is gone, and someone he knows is guilty. That's a lot of stress and pent-up anger. You can't prove what you know, I mean, what *he* knows, and that combination can make you nuts. It can make you do things you wouldn't normally do." Every pair of eyes is fixated on me, but I keep going as if ranting about Hamlet is just business as usual in the life of Nathan Boliva. "You don't even care what other people think, you just have to make things right."

The only sound is Jeremy's asthmatic breathing two seats behind me. Mrs. Barnes stares at me like I just sang the National Anthem with melodic perfection.

"Nathan, that was good." She sets her copy of *Hamlet* on the desk and sits down. "In fact, that was *amazingly* good. Far more passionate than I expected. Consider yourself exonerated from today's tardiness."

Really don't care, but I give her a nod, knowing my entire class thinks I'm as crazy as Shakespeare's Prince of Denmark.

Three classes later I'm heading down a hall where faces of trophied athletes stare at me from days gone by, many of them probably grandparents, some no longer of this world. Sean walks at a hurried pace in the opposite direction and signs *hi*, then crosses his eyes and makes a fish face. Normally this cracks me up, but I just keep going, wondering how a single morning can feel like days. Mitch and Matt, Alec's teammates, nod as I go by. I respond with a matching nod and a "Hey." Seems like they're bulking up lately, too, just like the best friend who hates me right now. Always thought they seemed a little shady and can't help wondering if they got him into something. I store it away to be revisited when Haylie is back to walking these halls with a smile that knocks me dead. It will happen. It *has* to.

"Hey, Nathan, wait up!" Veronica saunters toward me, thick eyeliner encircling blue eyes that might be pretty without their black frames. Auburn hair streaked with black hangs down her black tank top, grazing her chain link belt. Not many parents would see the genius behind the vampire get-up, but her Physics grades outshine Haylie's. And that's saying something. She reaches me and I know exactly what's coming.

"You hear about Haylie?"

"Yeah."

Raccoon eyes narrow to slits. "You know something. Speak."

One word, that's all I said. The FBI should have *her* interviewing suspects. "Nothing. I just meant I heard about it."

"You know more, but whatever. Can't believe this happened. One day she's sitting behind me in Physics, and then poof, she vanishes. Too weird. And kidnapped? Like what is *that* all about?"

"No idea. Pretty crazy." I keep it short, fearing an extra word or two will shine a spotlight on my feelings for Haylie.

"Yeah. Anyway, I figured you might know more about it, seeing you got the hots for her and all."

She tosses it out there like she's commenting on the weather. Humiliation rises to my face, settling in my ears, which are unfortunately visible thanks to my swimmer's haircut. My only strategy is to ignore the comment and focus on the kidnapping. "All I know is what's been on the news."

She purses her lips and nods. "Hey, maybe it's because her mom's a physicist, like in that movie where they capture the scientist to get the...oh, man! Gotta go. One more tardy and they'll send a letter home to Grams."

"Wait! To get the what?" But Veronica's already out of earshot, racing toward the art rooms while I stand in the hall like the blue plastic man in The Game of Life. The corridor veers off in one direction to the cafeteria and in the opposite to the outside doors. To ditch or not to ditch, that is the question. Leaving now would go against all that is right. I could get caught by Smirley, who seems to be everywhere. I'd be truant from school, which could bench me for next week's swim meet. And for what? How can I help Haylie, anyway? The only logical option is to head over to the cafeteria and see if Alec is willing to talk to me yet. At the crossroads, I look left and see the sun pouring in through the glass double doors. Haylie is out there somewhere. I turn in the direction of the only choice I can live with.

Chapter 9

Nathan
Friday Afternoon

Leaves crunch beneath my shoes as I jog up the steps and slip my key in the door. What can I possibly accomplish other than making everyone mad again? Cheerful barks and wagging tails greet me on the other side. Ruby looks up with a faint "woof" and a half-wag. It's the best she can do. At least my canine siblings are happy I'm home. My parents won't share their excitement, but thankfully that drama won't happen 'til later. Right now, I need to use every brain cell, every memory, every *everything* I've got inside to find Haylie and bring her back.

Step one, assess the situation.

Wild Things is too far and I'm without a car. My only option is a cab ride that would cost more than I've got. Mr. Summers probably wouldn't be there, anyway. Time to shift gears. Like Alessio said, even information that seems insignificant can help solve a case.

Step two, research. I grab my laptop.

ZetaLab's "About Us" page says it's a "government supported, high-energy physics research facility" about eight miles from Heron Lake. The details make my eyes glaze over. Something about examining the smallest building blocks of matter, which they call particle physics research, and understanding the intricacies of space and time. They find new ways to treat cancer and make scientific machines and instruments. There's a whole fact sheet about their work with dark matter and dark energy. And they work with scientists and engineers from dozens of other countries. My eyes are drawn to the stuff about developing super conducting magnets.

I picture Wile E. Coyote feeding metal pellets to Roadrunner, then using one of those giant horseshoe magnets to draw him in. Every metal object in the country flies toward my cartoon vision of the gigantic superconducting magnet. In reality, I can't imagine why anyone would need one, but apparently, I'm missing something.

I read further. Blah, blah, blah, 'Magnetic Resonance Imaging, also known as MRI.' Yeah, okay, those things they use to scan people's bodies in hospitals. Her mom must be pretty brainy to work at a place like that.

I flop onto my bed to analyze the information I've acquired in the past twenty-four hours. Today is Friday, and Haylie has been missing since Wednesday evening. It's definitely a kidnapping because there's a ransom note. Her stepdad is a wildlife vet and, as far as I'm concerned, a primary suspect, although Kimiko seems pretty convinced he's a good guy. There's nothing to say her mom can't be a suspect, too—there's some nasty moms out there. Monday's news had a mom who drowned her three kids in the bathtub. Wednesday's news had a mom who kept her son in a dog cage. Man, I'm glad I didn't get an insane mom.

But Haylie's mom can't be crazy. It doesn't fit that Haylie would be who she is with a psycho mom. Her intellect, her aura of confidence and vitality, that sparkle in her eyes, tells me she's not living day to day under the crush of physical or emotional abuse. Her mom is officially off my suspect list, which brings it back down to one. Two, if I count myself, which I don't, but the FBI apparently does. Just because of that stupid note and the text I didn't send.

That's everything. That's *nothing*. It's not enough to help me find Haylie, and there's just two hours left before Mom comes home and it all hits the fan. If I'm going to be in trouble, the next two hours better count.

Step three—

Rapid knocks jar me out of my investigative thoughts. There's no good reason for someone to be here on a weekday afternoon. Could be a salesman. Or Kingman, wanting to borrow our ladder again. But he knows our schedule all too well. I slither onto the floor and crawl to the window, peeking out from the side of the open blinds. The black car at the curb is disturbingly familiar. The top of Smirley's head greets me from my second floor window. He probably arranged for the school to contact him if I left. Will he break in if I don't answer? On the crime shows they always need a search warrant. I wait, cringing as he pounds the door three more times.

"FBI!" He lays the authority on thick. "Open up, Nate!"

Now I'm stuck. He's ruining my plan. Well, he would be…if I had one.

Hours tick by, although the clock shows it's only been three minutes. Smirley storms back to his car and takes off. No doubt he'll come around again to see if he can catch me leaving, but I didn't ditch school just to stick around the house all day.

Creeping out the mud room door, I crawl behind Mom's row of azaleas. Once the bushes end, I can cut across a twenty-foot open area to Kingsman's backyard bush, a monstrosity roughly the size of Rhode Island. Then a quick hop over his fence and across the other neighbor's yard to the next street, where Smirley won't think to look for me.

I reach the end of the azaleas and get ready to stand for the bush sprint.

"Hey there, Nathan!" Mr. Kingman is carrying a rake as he walks toward me. "Lose somethin'?"

My whole body cringes. "Well..."

"Beautiful day, isn't it?" Fortunately, Kingman is more into talking than listening. "I'm just about to do some rakin'." He tugs at a few leaves stuck to the end of his rake. "You know that old maple just keeps on droppin' those leaves."

"Well, it is October." I stand up, painfully conscious of how visible I am from just about every angle. Astronauts living in the space station can probably see me right now. "Don't let me stop you, Mr. Kingman. It's a great day to rake."

"Shouldn't you be in school?"

I crouch, pretending to look for something. Not that it'll do me any good at this point. "Got out early, but there's someplace I've got to go. Can't stay and talk. Sorry."

He leans on his rake and gets nice and comfortable. "Now, hold on there, Nathan. I got some news to share."

I try to contain my joy.

"I know where she goes."

"Who?"

"That Mrs. Vitalli with her Lily dog. I followed her this morning."

"You did?"

"Don't you worry. She didn't see me or nothin'. I was real sneaky about it. She walked over to that church two blocks down, over on Sky View Court." A breeze sends more leaves drifting onto his lawn, and he pauses to glare at them. "She tied up that dog under a shady tree and stayed in there for about fifteen minutes."

"You waited?"

"Well, it was only a short time, and the weather was nice."

The man's going to get himself arrested and have a heart attack in prison because his lawn isn't getting watered. "You know that's stalking, right? People tend to frown on that. A lot, actually."

"No, no, it wasn't nothin' like that. I was just following her and watchin', that's all."

"Oh, just following and watching and waiting for her to come out. Not stalking." I wonder, for the thousandth time, if other people have these kinds of conversations. It just doesn't seem possible.

"Exactly! So then she came out and got her dog and headed home. And that dang Lily dog walked right on my grass again, like maybe it hates me or somethin'."

And I'm beginning to understand why. "I don't think the dog hates you. Really. Dogs just walk on grass and don't really think about it."

"Could be. Still, a person's lawn is private property, know what I mean? Well, back to the rakin'. Those leaves aren't going to disappear on their own." He turns away, then back again. "You need help finding what you lost?"

"No, thanks. I don't think it matters much now."

And there goes my plan. I walk to the front of the house with "here I am!" flashing across my forehead in neon lights. As if on cue, a black car comes around the corner and pulls up to the curb. Perfect. Next time I'll just call ahead so he'll be waiting. The passenger side window opens to reveal Smirley at the wheel.

Please, God, make him evaporate. I'm not sure it's okay to pray like that, but definitely worth a try.

"Get in, Nate." No premise of friendliness this time.

"Why?"

"Mostly because I said so, but also because someone wants to talk to you."

"Who?" Dragging out the conversation with questions will, at the very least, delay entering that man's car.

"*Get in.* Unless you want this scenario to go downhill from here, which can happen pretty easily. Those cuffs can get awfully uncomfortable."

Not the answer I was looking for, but definitely

incentive for complying with his request. Once inside, I breathe in the aroma of leather and pine, knowing there's a little tree-shaped air freshener dangling somewhere. We ride in silence. I don't give him the satisfaction of asking where we're going, because he'll only use it to irritate me with more unnecessary sarcasm. I don't deserve that. Haylie definitely doesn't deserve whatever's happening to her, and neither does Ruby. With each spin of the tires, anger heats the blood sizzling through my veins. Anger at the kidnappers, Smirley, Kingman.

Anger at God. Where was his protection? His love? His miracles? Just *one* would be fine. One miracle.

We turn down Haylie's street. Maybe they found her, and she asked for me. Is it possible he wouldn't have told me? Yes. I swallow the microscopic fragment of pride I have left and force a casual tone. "So did you find Haylie?"

He continues staring straight ahead. "Do you *think* we found Haylie?"

I look at his smirky face and my fist clenches, but I rein it in. Cool the blood. For her. "I really don't know, sir. That's why I asked." Maybe he'll like the sir and answer like a human being.

He shakes his head. "No, Nate. We didn't find her. For *some* reason, her mother wants to talk to you. And for *some* reason, Alessio gave it the thumbs-up. I was on my way to your school when I got the call that you ditched."

So I was right. I nod, having nothing to contribute.

"You just cooperate. None of your little tricks, understand?"

I toy with the idea of saying I don't understand and could he please explain it a few more times, but really, what good would come of it? "Got it."

"We're keeping her stepdad in a separate room, as he's feeling a bit hostile toward you, if you catch my drift.

He's feeling hostile? I force myself to respond calmly so I don't sound like a maniac. "About what? I didn't do anything."

"So you say."

Unbelievable.

"Mrs. Summers is just as hostile, but agreed to hold her feelings in check because she wants to talk with you one on one."

I look out the window, where the trees of our local nature center whoosh by, and wish I could leap out the door and run into the woods. This meeting is going to be a nightmare.

Mrs. Summers bears little resemblance to the smiling, pretty woman in the family photo on the wall. Eyes puffy like Kimiko's, hair pulled back into a rubber band, and pale lips set in a stone-carved grimace. I extend my hand when Smirley introduces me, but she does not return the gesture. Awkward. He escorts us to the kitchen and leaves us alone to talk. Maybe I watch too many crime shows, but I can't help wondering if she's wired.

"I appreciate you meeting with me. I won't waste time with small talk." Clipped words come to me through clenched teeth.

Not sure of the proper response, I just go with "okay."

"Haylie is my daughter. I love her more than you could ever, *ever* imagine. I would do *anything* to get her back. I would give my life for her, do you understand?"

"Yes ma'am."

"I'm serious, Nathan. Do you?" Her eyes shoot bullets of hatred, but her voice remains calm.

"Yes, ma'am. I want her back too. It's all I think about."

"You may not know what the kidnappers want and their plans for it, but the text...it came from *your* phone." She points to me, probably wishing her finger was a gun. "And yes, I know you said it was stolen, but if you're lying..." She stops, closes her eyes, and puts her hand to her mouth. Tears squeeze past her eyelashes and stream down her cheeks. I want to say something, but my throat is tightening and nothing comes out.

She takes a breath and looks at me, eyes begging for something. But I've got nothing.

"If you had something to do with this, just tell me. Any tidbit that could lead us to her. Maybe they gave you money to send the text. Maybe you had no idea anything bad would happen to Haylie. I don't care." Her voice rises, seething with anger. She looks away and takes a deep breath before continuing. "You *must* tell me. Whatever you want in return, name it." Calmer now, her voice cracks. The pain in her eyes rips my guts right open. "I swear, I won't press charges. All I want in this world is my Haylie back."

She puts her hand on the table, leaning slightly, like an old lady with a walker.

You may not know what the kidnappers want and their plans for it.

The ransom note visualizes in my brain. Nothing in it even hinted at the cost of getting Haylie back. I shift gears, mentally zipping through my talks with the agents. Nothing. She's assuming I know.

She needs to know I'm not involved. I'm not that kind of person. But all the words that come to mind sound hollow and rehearsed. "I didn't do it, Mrs. Summers. I would never hurt Haylie. I don't know why anyone would want to."

She sits now, apparently needing full support. "The video made their reasons quite clear. But I can't give them what they want. I don't even have it anymore. The FBI has everything." She swipes her cheeks, places both hands on the table and locks her eyes on mine. "Do you know *anything*?"

How do I answer that? The only clue came from her own husband's mouth, and the FBI probably didn't even tell her. She may not believe me, but she needs to know the truth.

"You know something, Nathan. I see it in your eyes."

I sit down in the kitchen chair adjacent to her. "Yeah."

She leans in. "I'm listening."

"I like your daughter, Mrs. Summers. I don't know her very well yet, but I still like her. We had a pizza date for today after school."

"I know. Haylie was really looking forward to it. Go on."

"After the FBI questioned me, I snuck out to snoop around your house. I'm really sorry. I had to do something. It was all I could think of."

"We're already aware of that. What do you know?"

I recap the brief conversation, word for word, as best I remember, and wait for her reaction. Might be anger, more tears, denial, confusion. Anything is possible. Anything but the sad little smile that crosses her lips.

"I already know about this. Russell was talking to his assistant at Wild Things. It's the rescue center where he works." Mrs. Summers leans back and deflates with a sigh. Her glimmer of hope has been snuffed by useless information. "He and Haylie have been working with a gorilla there, Imani, teaching her to sign. But since neither one of them has been around for a couple of days, Imani was getting upset. The assistant called him late that night because Imani was trying to communicate something. She was agitated. That's the conversation you overheard."

"Oh." My one great piece of information, my save-the-day blockbuster, was about a gorilla.

"Is that it, Nathan? Anything else?"

"No. Sorry." I almost want to make up something, just to fix a little part of her brokenness.

She sniffs and runs her fingers through wheat-colored hair. Kinda like Haylie's, but with random strands of gray. I've given her no hope whatsoever. "But if it matters, I'll keep trying to think of anything that could help."

"Thank you."

She needs more than that, I can tell. "And my whole church is praying for her." As soon as I say it, I remember

I don't know what Haylie believes in and maybe that doesn't matter at all to Mrs. Summers, but the words are already out.

Her eyes soften. "Really? Thank you. We're doing a lot of that here as well. You keep it up, okay?" Her lips curve into a sad smile, but it's better than the cold glare from the woman who wouldn't shake my hand. "I told those agents I needed to meet you. To see for myself if you were in on this. I thought I'd be able to tell. Turns out, I was right. You can tell a lot from looking in a person's eyes, don't you think?"

Too bad Smirley doesn't share her instincts. "I do, and thanks. I hope Mr. Summers will believe it too."

"Well… at the moment he'd like to roll you in ground meat and dump you in the tiger pen, but I'll talk to him."

Not how I wanted Haylie's dad to feel about me, but that's the least of my problems right now. It's also a really horrible—and weirdly creative—way to dispose of someone.

Mrs. Summers gets up and folds a kitchen towel that's draped over a chair. "They've asked me a million questions." She picks up the towel and folds it again, then pats it several times. "Questions about Haylie and her friends, *my* family and friends, even my coworkers. But honestly, I work with the nicest group of people." She holds the towel against her, Linus style. "In fact, one of the men I've worked with for years has a daughter Haylie's age. Sometimes we compare notes, you know, like parents do. I even told him she had a date with a boy from the swim team. He said he knows a guy on the team and asked your name, but it wasn't you." Silence thickens the air between us. She looks out toward a vegetable garden beyond the deck, where dying tomato plants lean over like old men. "Anyway, I just don't know anyone that would do this. It's beyond crazy."

We walk out and Mrs. Summers places her hand on my back. "Thanks, Nathan," she says. "I'm glad we talked."

Smirley rolls his eyes. Someone liking me must make the bile rise in his throat. "All right, let's get you back to school, which is where you were supposed to be in the first place."

We head toward the door and his phone goes off. He flicks it open. "Smirley." A short pause, then "Hi, Doc, hold on one second." He turns to me. "Wait out back. I need a few minutes here. And stay put."

For once my mind controls my mouth and the words "you're a moron" stay silenced. I wait for him on Haylie's cedar deck. There are a couple of blue striped lounge chairs, the good padded kind you can sink into and fall asleep, but I remain standing and pace, mentally going over my conversation with Mrs. Summers.

"Hey."

The nasal voice comes from the next yard. I turn to see a guy leaning on the black metal fence. His shoulder-length hair hasn't touched shampoo in days. Maybe longer. A Rolling Stones T-shirt complete with a faded outline of big red lips drapes his skinny frame like a tent. He seems to be a few years older than me. I hear Alec's voice in my head, laughing as he says, "The eighties called and want you back," but curiosity draws me toward him.

"Yeah?" I stop about two feet from the fence.

He leans forward, squints, and points to me. "You take Haylie?"

"No, man, I'm her friend. I didn't take her."

He wipes his nose with his bare hand. "Yeah, well it's funny how you came around the same time she disappeared."

My ears stand at attention. "What are you talking about?" I step closer and catch the musty sweet scent of weed.

"I saw you drive by real slow on Wednesday." He scratches the scorpion tattoo on his arm. "Then, a little while later, Haylie was hangin' out back and you returned with some other dudes in masks and grabbed her. I saw you, man."

My head spins. What the heck is he talking about? Yeah, I cruised by her house before dinner, but then I left. Lame, yes. Criminal, no. "I just came by once. I didn't come back."

"Yeah, right. Same car, except for that Chicago Bears sticker on the rear window."

I have so many questions, so little time, and no idea if whatever he knows is even remotely valid. "You're saying a car that looked like mine, with a Bears decal, came here?"

He bobs his head. "Yep and yep."

"And some guys in masks got out and took Haylie?"

Another nod.

"Didn't they see you?"

More scratching. It's a miracle that tattoo is still visible. "Nah. I was hidin' in that corner by the garage." He raises his thumb and index finger to his lips and makes an exaggerated inhaling noise. "It's my happy place, know what I mean?"

Does he know that's legal now? Doesn't matter. That revelation could completely derail this discussion and I'm not risking it."

"Yeah, I get it. Did you tell the cops what you saw?"

"Nah."

"Why not?"

He shrugs. "Why should I? For all I knew, it could have been a joke or somethin'. Then later I fell asleep, you know? Didn't really think about it 'til those guys came around with all their questions."

I'm dumbfounded. And skeptical. "Did you hear them talk? The guys that took Haylie?"

"Man, dude, you got a lot of questions, too. So, like, why should I tell you anything? For all I know, you're in on it."

"Look, it wasn't me. I swear I just want to find her

before someone hurts her." He reminds me of the
squirrel I used to feed a few years back. If I stayed very
still, it would take a peanut out of my hand, but one
wrong move and it would scurry off.

"Oh, man, like, you think someone would hurt her?"
This comes as a complete surprise to him. "Not cool, man.
Not cool at all. She's a sweetheart. Deaf, you know. Can't
hear a thing." He contemplates a dried bit of food on his
beloved T-shirt and picks it off.

I've got to get this guy talking to me. He obviously saw
something and I want to find out more before Smirley
kills the moment. It comes to me like a gift from above.

"Great shirt, by the way. Keith Richards is awesome on
guitar. Maybe even the best ever." Dad has an old Stones
album in his room. Kept it all these years. I remember the
title and use this to my advantage. "How about 'Wild
Horses'—is that cool or what?" I silently beg him to say
he's heard of it. It's the only one I remember.

"Oh, man, yeah!"

He takes the bait. "How about 'Hot Rocks?' Burnout
Neighbor Guy breaks into air guitar mode. "That's like,
my fave."

Never heard of it. "Oh, yeah, I know what you mean." I
hope my enthusiasm sounds at least remotely authentic.
Maybe he'll open up now that we're fellow Rolling Stones
groupies. "Listen, before the agent comes out, can you tell
me if those guys said anything?"

"What guys?"

Focus here, buddy. Focus. "Those guys that took
Haylie. The guys in the masks."

"Oh, *those* guys? Hmmm." He actually scratches his
head like Shaggy from the Scooby Doo cartoons, eyes
squeezed tight. "Hmm. I'm thinkin'."

I could have graduated and gotten married in the time
it takes him to think about it.

"Meet us at sunset."

"Meet us at sunset? One of the guys said that?"

He nods.

"Anything else? Did they say *where*?"

"Nah. That's it, man. I got nothin' else. And hey, don't rat me out, okay?" His eyes scan the yard. "They don't need to know that came from me."

"I won't. Thanks. That was ..." The back door squeaks and Burnout Neighbor Guy scampers to his garage like he's being hunted by an eagle.

"Well, Nate, make a new friend, did we?" Smirley struts over toward me, shoving his cell into his pocket. "The two of you have a nice little chat?"

I don't want to tell this guy what I know, but I have to tell somebody because it might help Haylie.

"No clever comebacks for me today? I'm disappointed." Hands in pockets, his eyes pierce me like little switchblades.

A car door slams and I look between the houses to see a welcome face emerging from a black sedan. Agent Alessio starts toward the front door, then spots me and Smirley in the backyard and changes direction. Now I can give *her* a description of the car with the Bears sticker. From the yard next door, Burnout Neighbor Guy holds his finger to his lips, eyes begging me not to "rat him out."

"Hello, Nathan. Did you talk to Haylie's mother?"

"Yes. She believes I'm not involved."

Smirley pulls out his car keys. "Yeah, she seems to think he's Mr. Innocent now. I've got an Uber coming to take him to school. The hospital called. I need to get over there. Sorry."

"No apologies, Carl. You go. Tell Nadia I said hello."

"Thanks. She loved the flowers you sent."

A car pulls up to the curb and Smirley turns to me. "Your ride's here."

I pause, watching Alessio head into the house as Smirley glares at me, gesturing for me to get in. Haylie got into a Camry with a Chicago Bears sticker. This is important. Someone needs to know. I open my mouth to tell the jerk standing next to me.

"What's your problem? Get in, already! I have someplace to be." I step into the Uber with the new information tucked safely away in my head, wondering if I was just handed the key to finding Haylie.

Chapter 10

Haylie
Two months ago

Mom is reading in the living room, the scent of our salmon dinner still wafting on the air, mixing with the sea-breeze candle she hopes will vanquish it. I sit down next to her and she lays the book in her lap, turning to face me.

"I want to meet him." My words hold more conviction this time. The thought had ambled around my head over the years, but in the end, fear always won out. He hadn't wanted me back then, when I was a three-year-old who adored him, so why would he want to see me now? But yesterday changed everything.

"Oh, honey. This again?" She didn't need to ask who I was talking about. "Is it because of Kimiko's dad? The heart attack?"

He'd almost died. When I drove Kimiko to the hospital yesterday, I hardly recognized the man. He lay there in that hospital bed, weak and frail because one tiny little clot prevented blood from flowing to his heart. Kimiko held his hand and cried. As I watched them, life became fragile; a dandelion caught in a wind that steals its silken puffs. I realized I didn't want mine, or my father's, to end without knowing the truth.

"It's time. I don't know what will happen, but I need to find out. I don't want him in my life, but I want to know why he left us. Why he wouldn't try counseling. Why he stopped coming to see me. I want to hear it from *him*."

"We've talked about this. The man is a mess. Gambling, alcohol, losing job after job. You know all this."

I do. We've had the talk more than once. There's the romantic part, where they met at a local art fair when she was admiring his photos. "I'm in marketing Monday through Friday," he told her, "but on weekends, I do what I love." He gestured toward his nature photos. "This." Six months later, they married in a sunset ceremony in Colorado Springs. When I was born, they were "over the moon." That's how she says it. Every time. *We were over the moon about our little fairy princess.* And then the news. The princess is deaf. Tears, stress, doctor appointments, arguments over medical and lifestyle decisions.

"Tell me again." It's a mantra she's heard before. Her answer will remind me that my father didn't leave because I was deaf, but the reassurance is temporary. A conviction that fades away as time goes by and the little voice in my head whispers "it was all because of you." When the whispers become shouts, I come to her and say the words that have become a painfully familiar part of our existence. "Tell me again." And so she does.

"Start with the boat."

She cups my hand in both of hers, and I see the hint of pain shade her face, but she lets go and raises her hands to sign.

"It was just before your second birthday. We hadn't gone out as a couple since you were born. My coworker, Rob, invited us for an evening on a gambling boat, saying it would be good for us to have a night out, so we went." She slips her bookmark into her paperback and sets it on the coffee table. "I wasn't impressed. Too smoky and noisy. Too many lights. Too much money being thrown away. His wife didn't seem to like it much, either."

But my father saw it with a different set of eyes. She continues the story, explaining, as always, that he went back with Rob the following week, and several times after that. When Rob switched to the racetrack, my father would go to the boat alone. Mom suspected it was more than once a week. He'd come home late from work, saying he had "important projects," but there was no extra money in his paycheck from working all those extra hours.

"Our bank account was dwindling. I'd question him; he'd get defensive. He even tried to pin it on your medical expenses."

Arguments ensued. Long talks. Promises were made. And broken. Made again. And broken again. He didn't even go to sign language classes with her. He was too busy "working."

"By the time you were three, I couldn't take it anymore. I was done, and he was out. For the next few months he came to see you every week. Then every other week. Once a month, and then--"

I take her hands and move them down to her lap. She doesn't have to be the one to say it. "Then nothing."

It must have been lonely in that dark place, wondering what happened; why the man who'd brought her such joy turned out to be her greatest sorrow. And there she was with a deaf child and no one to share the challenges. Until our visit to the Wild Things Rescue Shelter.

"Remember when we met New Dad?" We laugh at the nickname I had for him when they first got married.

She nods. "Your fifth birthday. I wanted to give you a pool party, but even then, Wild Things was your favorite place in the whole world."

Dr. Russell Summers was returning a young cheetah to her pen when he saw us, walked over, and started signing. In that moment, a light illuminated the darkness my father had cast over us.

"You never questioned his ability to sign; just interrogated him about the cheetah, and told him it was your birthday, of course."

We ate the "birthday ice cream" he bought us in the pretty courtyard next to the concession stand. Two years later, we returned, but this time I was wearing a sparkly blue dress and Mom was in white. Dr. Russell Summers became Dad with his "I do," and all my animal friends got to witness the best day of our lives.

We sit without speaking, each lost in our thoughts. Meeting Dad that day was nothing short of a miracle, for which I'll be forever grateful. Mom's transformation was obvious, even to a child. She worried less and smiled a whole lot more. He brought laughter and stability to our lives and opened my eyes to the plight of wildlife worldwide. And he instilled in me a passion that I hope will become a career.

But lately, questions about my bio father have taken root in me, growing and blooming until they fill my head. Mom has always been great about telling me what happened without any animosity tainting her words, but it's not enough anymore. This time, I want the answers to come from the man who left us.

"Can you find him?"

She nods. "I think my coworker is still in touch with him from time to time. Rob, the one who used to go to the casino with him. I'll ask."

————

Mom pulls up in front of Burger Bill's Grill, where we wait in the parking lot for my bio father to meet us. She turns off the car and we look around at the unfamiliar neighborhood, an hour south of ours, where graffiti mars the side of every building. Plastic bags catch a breeze and roll along the street like urban tumbleweeds. A used syringe lies on the ground, a few inches from a condom.

Also used. I try not to think about how it got there. A few feet from our car, a homeless man lying on a bus stop bench sits up to scratch his butt, then returns to sleep.

"I don't like this," Mom signs. "Not at all."

"Really? You don't want to move into that vacant house down the street?"

She rolls her eyes. "I'm just saying I don't feel good about leaving you in this place."

She's not the only one who's not feeling good. The nausea started when we left the house and hit like a tidal wave when we pulled into this lot. And the trembling. I've spent hours with tigers, cheetahs and a gorilla who could rip me apart in seconds, and never trembled like this. I just want to be angry. That's all. One emotion. With all he's done…and hasn't done…it's the only one that makes sense. He's the one who should be nervous. He's the one who should be worried that this meeting is going to be an epic disaster. And yet…

"We're here, though. Let's just wait and see." I can't chicken out now, not after all the years of having imaginary conversations with him. In most of them, I end up walking away and saying I never want to see him again. But every now and then, for reasons I can't comprehend, it doesn't end that way at all.

"He might not show up."

This isn't helping. She thinks she's protecting my heart with her warnings, but her words only take my anxiety to a higher level. "So you've said. A hundred times." I text Kimiko while we wait and she sends a laughing emoji when I tell her it's a burger joint.

Just tell him you're not a carnivore. Maybe they have tofu or salads or something.

I open the window and snap a photo of the streaked window painted with a giant burger and a tattered menu taped to the door. Unreadable from this distance, but she'll get the point. I send it and two seconds later my phone lights up.

Yikes. Kimiko adds the shocked face emoji that always makes me laugh.

Doesn't matter. So not hungry.

Stay strong. Her words are followed by a muscled arm. That girl loves her emojis. You got this.

Not so sure. I wait for her next response while Mom surveys the neighborhood to make sure no one sneaks up on us.

You hang out with TIGERS and a giant GORILLA! Remember who you are! (Didn't mean to sound like Mufasa.) Naturally, she follows this up with a lion face. If you don't like how it's going, just leave. You're the one who was wronged. You're the one in control.

Mom touches my arm to get my attention and points out the window. A man approaches. Honey blond hair that matches mine. Skinny. Gray hoodie. Jeans nearly faded to white at the knees. I forget how to breathe, how to move, how to think. I forget how to feel angry. But I don't forget how to tremble. That function still works perfectly.

He's here. I send the text to Kimiko and tuck my phone into my pocket.

Mom gets out of the car. I hesitate, then do the same. No one smiles. I step closer and watch his face, not wanting to miss a word.

"Hello, Olivia," he says to Mom. "Thank you for bringing her. Really. That means a lot."

"You're welcome." She signs as she talks to him. "It's just for an hour, unless she wants to end it sooner."

He turns to me, eyes shimmering. "Look at you. So beautiful."

Our eyes connect. My throat thickens. He's here. Right here in front of me. Hurt rises, filling the place where anger is supposed to be firmly planted. All the years of picturing this moment never prepared me for this. He shouldn't have the power to unveil my hurt, or any emotions outside the arena of anger and resentment. He keeps looking in my eyes, seeing the pain inside, and I hate it. I was going to show him I'm fine without him. Didn't need him. Life is good. But all I can do is stand here, struggling to breathe, and wishing I were a million miles away. I turn around and get back into the car. In a heartbeat, the driver side door opens and Mom slides in.

"If you want to leave, that's fine," she signs. "Is that what you want?"

I shake my head. There's no turning back now.

"Do you want me to stay?"

Another shake. I need to make this happen, whatever it takes. "No. It's got to be just me and him."

"You're sure?"

"Yes." I just want to hate him, that's all. Or, even better, feel nothing.

"Okay." Worry veils her eyes. "He knows to give you his phone number right away, so you can talk through text."

I nod, but she already knows I know the plan. We sit without talking while my father stands awkwardly next to the car. I open the window for fresh air and breathe deep, but my yoga instructor's "works every time" calming strategy fails miserably as I'm assaulted by the aroma of greasy meat. There may be a way for this moment to get worse, but I can't begin to imagination such a scenario. The thought of sharing this travesty with Kimiko almost makes me laugh. Almost. Or maybe it was a dry heave. Mom pats my thigh and asks if I need anything. "A big fat prayer," I say, because nothing less is going to get me through the next hour.

"I'm on it," she says.

Movement catches my attention. My dad is walking away. After three minutes of me sitting here, he's leaving. Again. After everything, he couldn't just wait a few minutes for me to get it together. Anger finally returns, curling its inky tendrils around my heart and diminishing the nausea. My trembles cease as he approaches the

bench and taps the homeless man on the shoulder. When
the man turns and sees my father, his eyes light with
recognition. He smiles, sits up, and the two shake hands
like old friends. Mom and I watch the exchange unfold
like audience members in a theater. They talk briefly
before my father hands the man a couple of dollars and
returns to the car.

The hate betrays me yet again, slinking back to its
hiding spot.

"Take your time," he says through the window, then
grabs a tiny bottle of hand sanitizer from his pocket and
drips it into his palm.

I take another deep breath, forcing myself to ignore
the powerful scent of fried cows. The reunion I've wanted
for years is one "hello" away, and I'm consumed by
emotions that were not invited to this party. But this is
not the "me" he's going to see.

Mom's fingertips gently lift my chin. "Remember why
you're here. Maybe that will help. Think about what you
want to tell him."

I replay the conversation I've conjured a million times
in my head while running, lying in bed, showering. In
those perfect conversations, words flow like a literary
river. I tell him he shattered my little-girl heart, that I was
angry at Mom for sending him away, and later, drowning
in guilt because I thought his leaving was my fault. I
hated being deaf, thinking he might have stayed if I were
"normal." But that's behind me now, and I'll tell him that,
too. Because I love being deaf, and have the greatest
friends in the Deaf Community. This is who I am. An
honor roll student, a runner, an animal advocate. A
person who loves deeply and hurts deeply and is willing
to fight for what's right. Daughter of Olivia and Russel
Summers, big sister to the coolest little brother on the
planet. Child of God, who loves me unconditionally and
made me all these things. And after my father knows
what he caused, and what he missed, I'll ask my

questions, demand answers, and be done with him.

I glance out the window and see him sitting on an old plastic crate against the restaurant's brick wall. Head in hands, he stares at the gravel. A man who had it all and lost it all. Not by war or oppression or circumstances beyond his control, but through weakness, greed, selfishness. These thoughts bring me clarity, and clarity gives way to sparks of strength. By the time I leave, he'll know he's nothing but a loser who missed out on a great life with me and Mom.

The sparks flicker and dance, brightening into tiny flames of courage.

When I emerge from that grease pit restaurant, I'll finally be able to move forward with school and relationships and Wild Things, minus the anger and resentment that's plagued me since that man on the crate walked out of my life. But none of that can happen if I don't get my butt out of this car.

The flames blaze into an inferno. I turn toward Mom.

"I'm ready." I grab the door handle.

She touches my cheek. "Yes, you are. I can see it in your eyes."

"See you in an hour."

She leans in and hugs me. "Text if you want me back sooner. I'll be nearby."

My father waits for her to drive away before standing and walking toward me. We face each other on the crumbling pavement of that parking lot, neither knowing how to proceed. The prodigal father gazes like I'm a phenomenon he can't process. I motion toward the restaurant and take a step, afraid waiting a second more might prompt him to hug me. Once we're seated, he hands me a letter and signs, "Please read." He surprises me, but it's clear from the effort that he's far from fluent. When I'm done with his stupid letter, I'll tell him exactly what I just replayed in my mind and make it clear this meeting is a one-time thing. He can go back to his gambling or whatever else he does and keep his toxic self far away from me and Mom. I open the folded paper.

My Dear Haylie,

I love you more than words can say.

Liar. Those simple words send heat radiating through my body, rising to my neck. My face. How dare he. Does he think I'm that gullible? But I can't suppress the flicker of hope that buried in the lie is a fragment, however tiny, of truth. My throat thickens. I take a breath and stifle the emotions so I can get through this letter.

It's important you know that first, before I write anything else. I never stopped loving you. There's no excuse for the gambling that stole me away from you and all the incredibly stupid life choices that kept me from returning. You and your mom were the brightest lights in my life. I know you must have wondered why, but there's no logical answer when a person has an addiction. My life went downhill fast. Even when I thought about coming back, I was too mired in shame and guilt to have you and your mom see the mess that was me. I couldn't bring my darkness into your world.

A waitress stops by with water, menus, and a basket of rolls that look surprisingly fresh. Under normal circumstances, their warmth and buttery aroma would have been tempting.

I don't expect you to forgive me, and don't deserve it, but I can hope. And I can pray for it – something I've just recently started doing again. God showed me he's still in the business of working miracles when your mom called about meeting you.

It's been almost a year since I've stopped drinking and gambling. It's not a guarantee of anything, but I'm trying, with the help of a great support group.

I've been learning sign language, but I'm not so

great at it, so it would have been hard to say all these things. My plan was to call you on Christmas, but when your mom called, Christmas came three months early.

The waitress returns to take our orders. My father smiles and asks her to give us some time. His lips are easy to read, which isn't the case with everyone. It will help make up for his lack of signing skills.

Please don't think this is creepy, but I search your name sometimes to see what you're doing. You are an amazing young woman, and I am incredibly proud of you.

I love you, Haylie. If there is any chance of forgiveness and reconciliation, I'm willing to do whatever it takes and wait as long as it takes.

Does he think his pretty little letter makes up for abandoning me? That tender words and regret will erase years of heartache? I draw in a breath, then another. My brain tries in vain to define the feelings sweeping over me. This was not the plan. This meeting was supposed to be the final chapter; my chance to slam the book closed. Forever. And here he is - this skinny, ragged, poor excuse for a father - handing me a new book and wanting me to open it to Chapter One.

And against all that makes sense and all the reasons not to...my heart betrays my convictions...and considers that possibility. But only for a fraction of a second, because that nonsense won't lead to anything good.

Chapter 11

Nathan
Friday Afternoon

Back in class, Mr. Saccaro is discussing the Vietnam War, a topic the news nerd in me would have normally found interesting. Not today, though, when all I can focus on is the clock. One hour and forty-five minutes until I can break out of this place and follow up on my clues. Sunset. Silver Camry. Chicago Bears sticker. But without a location, none of it does me any good. And I don't even know whether my source is remotely reliable.

If Haylie's life depends on what I know, she's dead for sure.

Next to me, Ethan from swim team sits engrossed in every word. His uncle lost a leg in that war and now he's a Kentucky senator. I know because Ethan's told me three times since we started this unit. Mr. Saccaro is winding up a chapter on the long-lasting negative impacts of the war.

"Nearly 40,000 people have been killed, and even more injured, by unexploded bombs and landmines hidden just inches below the ground's surface. That number would be significantly higher if not for the selfless work of great organizations, including veterans' groups, who've removed many of them before they had a chance to hurt someone."

Those North Vietnamese guys were smart killers, I'll give them that. Since they didn't care much about wiping out countless innocent civilians, they hid their deadly devices in plain sight. You could be standing in a field, inches away from a fatal blast, and not see it coming until you stepped on it.

Is Haylie in plain sight? So close I could walk to where she's hidden? It's happened before. A shoe salesman kidnapped a girl and kept her in his basement just blocks away from her house. He had her for years before she figured out a way to escape.

"See?" Ethan whispers. "They put those things everywhere. The one that got my uncle was in a rice paddy. Just below the surface, like he said."

I nod my head and check the clock, trying to look normal but feeling like there's a landmine under my skin and it's about to explode. Ten more minutes of Social Studies, then I can meet up with Alec in Spanish, our "easy A" class. I've got to convince him to talk to me. If I don't talk to somebody about all that's happened this morning and all these thoughts bouncing around my head, I'll detonate for sure. And Alec's the only somebody I can tell.

He's waiting just outside the classroom door with a glare that tells me the silent treatment is about to be replaced by a tirade. Right now, it's the better option, because then we can move forward.

"Where have you been? What is *wrong* with you?" His eyes spit fire at me, but he's talking. I can work with that. "They called me down to the principal, asking all these questions. And guess what? I didn't know *any* of the answers because you didn't tell me *anything*." The fire becomes an ember. Still furious, but releasing the anger as he speaks. After all these years, I know the drill. "No one believed me. Thanks, Nathan. It was like 'Sixty

Minutes' in there. You could have told me you were leaving. You could have told me *something*."

"I'm sorry. Seriously. I'll tell you everything after Spanish."

"You know what? Too late. I don't care. Go do whatever and leave me out of it."

One minute till the bell rings. One minute to get him back in my corner so he can help me scrutinize the clues and come up with something meaningful. Something that will bring help one step closer to Haylie. I glance down, the universal expression for regret, and apologize again in a softer voice, then meet his eyes. "Alec, please. I never expected last night to go the way it did. You know that. This thing with Haylie…it's killin' me."

It's working. Maybe because it's true. The ember in his gaze is diminishing. "And I'm really sorry you got in trouble."

"Ah, I'm over it. Just don't expect to see me much."

Mitch and Matt walk by and nod to Alec. He returns the gesture. They're either in on the Saturday afternoon mystery, or they know about it. There's no reason for my certainty, but I can't deny my suspicions. When Haylie is back home and life returns to normal, I'm going to find out what's going on and how they're connected if it's the last thing I do.

"I'll practically be living at the bakery. Goin' there today, in fact, and no doubt he'll keep me for clean-up."

The Channings clean The English Bakery every night like a regiment of Merry Maids. You can't find a single fingerprint on those glass pastry cases or a grain of sugar on the counter. Step by step, same procedure each time. I helped enough over the years to know. It's been awhile, but it looks might I may be joining the clean-up party tonight. It's the least I can do, and from a purely selfish motive, it might help take my mind off the kidnapping.

Like that's possible.

"I'll come by later and help. I'm busy after school, but

I'll be there for clean-up."

Señor Martinez strides down the hall and through the door with a "*vámonos, chicos*" and we turn to follow. I can fill Alec in on the day's events when we walk to our lockers after class.

———

The bell rings just as I finish writing down the homework assignment. Alec and I join up in the hall and talk about my "great escape" that became an epic failure, my talk with Mrs. Summers, and the unexpected visit with Burnout Neighbor Guy.

"Sorry I missed that last one. Would've been way better than taking the econ test."

"How'd you do?" I hope for an answer that will keep him on the soccer team. One more "D" in econ and he'll get benched...which would crush him.

He shrugs. "Don't know. Let's talk about you, though. For once, your life is way more interesting."

I tell him I don't know if any of the information I have is useful, and, of course, I say that Smirley was a jerk again.

"That bloke's right dodgy, if you ask me."

"No kidding. So all I know is these guys met up at sunset on Wednesday, but I don't know *where*." We reach our lockers and take what we need for tonight. "Anyway, I've got Alessio's phone number at home. I'll call her. If only I had a location."

We walk in silence to the bus and get on, sitting together this time. Alec stares out the window as we pass a strip of storefronts ending with a women's workout center. He turns to face me, eyes wide. "Maybe that *is* the location."

"What? Wanda's Workout World?"

He shoves me half out of my seat. "Yeah, Nathan. Maybe they're forcing her to take nonstop aerobics classes."

"All right, all right. *What* then?"

"Sunset. Maybe it's a place, not a time. When we went to Florida, Mum spent an afternoon at the Sunset Spa. There's probably other places with that name, too."

"You could actually be right."

He grins, all proud because he thought of something I didn't. "It's brilliant, and you know it. Come on, admit it."

"Fine. It's brilliant. *You're* brilliant. But only if you're right." I reach into my backpack for my phone, then groan as I remember it's gone. "Look up some Sunset places." My mind goes into sunset overload while I wait for Alec to grab his phone. Which he doesn't.

"Sorry, mate. Phone died at lunch."

"Of course it did." My mind zeroes in on every store, restaurant, dry cleaners—anyplace I've ever seen during the past seventeen years.

Alec slaps his thigh. "There's Sunset Bay Tanning Salon. Cat went there a couple of times."

"Really?" I always thought the tan was just part of the Cat phenomena. "Not likely they'd use a tanning salon, though." As soon as the words leave my mouth, another Sunset name hits me. "Remember the cruise we took on Lake Michigan after prom? Sunset Cruise, right? I still have the stupid plastic cup from the boat."

Alec shakes his head. "The cruise returns to the same spot it left from, so what would be the point?"

"True."

Alec's eyes open wide enough for me to see the light of a fresh thought. "You know what, mate? We're forgetting something. They grabbed her *after* sunset Wednesday night. That means—"

"It *could* still be the time, not the location. But if that's the case...sunset on which day? Might have been yesterday, or even tonight." Resolving the clue just rose to a higher level of urgency. Three hours 'til sunset. Will something happen to Haylie in three hours? Speculations consume me. They'll kill her? Put her on a plane? Sell her? I've got to talk to Alessio, and barring that, Smirley. My dislike for him is ridiculously insignificant compared with whatever might happen to Haylie.

"It could still be a place, though. Don't forget that."

Alec's right. We can't assume anything at this point.

We jump off the bus and I race toward the house, contemplating the string of tasks ahead. All I want to do is search for Sunset places, but Ruby needs her meds and they both need to go out and then get fed. I've got to call Agent Alessio and *then* I can try to figure out Sunset. But there's Kingman, hose in hand, just waiting to ambush me. Don't even think it about it, old man. Don't say a word; just keep watering your grass.

"Hey there, Nathan."

My life is a nightmare. "Hey, Mr. K. I'm kinda in a hurry today." I keep moving, knowing if I pause, it's over. My strategy fails miserably.

"Now hold on, hold on. You're always in such a hurry, but you'll want to hear this. I saw her again today. Even petted that Lily dog. She's not so bad, you know?"

I wasn't going to prolong the conversation by asking if he meant the dog or Mrs. Vitalli. "That's great, Mr. Kingman. See you later."

"No, no, wait. This will just take a second. You have to hear the rest."

No, really, I don't. I sooo don't, but I wait for him to continue.

"I followed her to that church again, but this time I peeked inside. She was just sittin' there quietly. There wasn't even a service goin' on. Kinda weird, huh? So then I went by that Lily dog and she stood up and wagged her tail like she was happy or somethin'. That dog's as weird as her owner, I tell ya. So, I just patted her a bit and went on home."

Big day at the Kingman house. No wonder he was waiting for me. This was more action than he'd seen in years. But why is he following Mrs. Vitalli? Is he actually going to yell at her because Lily walks on his lawn? And then it hits me. Man, I'm dense.

"So, Mr. Kingman, are you interested in Mrs. Vitalli?"

He nearly drops his hose, no small matter since it would have crushed an untold number of delicate grass seedlings. "*Interested*? Now what kind of question is that, Nathan?" He laughs. "*Interested*? I'm not some high school kid like you." He laughs harder, like someone who's just heard a bad joke and is trying hard to pretend it's funny.

I can't take this anymore, and though I hate to be rude to the old guy, there was never a better excuse for it.

"Sorry. Guess I was wrong about that. Anyway, like I said, I gotta go. See ya."

"Now just wait, young man. Seems to me you need to slow down now and again."

Maybe it's the stress, or just sheer desperation, but for whatever reason, I come right out with it in hopes the truth will set me free...so to speak. "Mr. K., you know the girl that's missing? Haylie Summers?"

"Oh sure, sure. I heard it on the news. Terrible thing. What's this world coming to?"

Now there's a question...one I can't begin to delve into right now. "I know her. We go to school together. I have a clue that could lead to where she is and I really have to figure it out, you know? So, I *have* to go now."

He turns off the hose. Wrinkles furrow his forehead. "Run it past me, boy. I'm good with clues. I always figure out who dunnit on those SCI shows."

"CSI."

"That's what I said. Come on now, out with it."

That's actually not a bad idea. He can chew on it while I escape into my house. "Sunset. That's the clue. But I don't think they meant it like dusk, I think it might be a place." I start backing away again. "So, let me know if you think of anything, Mr. K. See ya."

I turn my back, secure in knowing he'll still be mulling

it over long after I shut my front door.

"Like the old Sunset Inn over there on River Road?"

His words fly out the minute I take a step, freezing my leg in mid stride.

"What?" I do an about-face, sure I must have heard wrong.

"That abandoned motel not far from the sammich place. Sunset Inn. Remember? I told you my nephew's crew is gonna demolish it and build a new place in a couple weeks. I don't know why they allow Kyle to have that ponytail, though. Seems to me it could get caught in somethin' and – "

"Mr. Kingman!" I didn't mean to startle him, but this was no time for a social commentary on men's hair.

Kingman's bushy gray eyebrows arch over bulging eyes, then return to normal. "Sorry, Nathan. Guess I got carried away. Now, where was I? Oh yeah, yeah, Sunset Inn. Near the corner of River Road and .... Hmm. Let me think. River Road and somethin'. I picked up Kyle there a few weeks back when his car died." He shakes his finger as though Kyle is standing in front of him. "You know, if he'd just take care of the thing it wouldn't keep breakin' down. He probably hasn't changed the oil in a year. Now, where was I? Oh yes, I took River and can't picture what the crossroad was. It'll come to me in a minute."

My head will likely explode before that happens.

"Peterson, I believe. Yes, that's it. Peterson. I remember now cuz Kyle's last name is Peters and I thought it was funny that Kyle *Peters* was gonna be workin' on *Peterson* Street. Ha! But see that? It helped me remember. Funny how things work out."

Calling out my thanks, I run to the house and try to quickly let the dogs out, but Ruby struggles to get up. I half carry her to the back door, frustrated by the delay and hating myself for feeling that frustration when my sweet dog is fading away before my eyes. While they're outside, I look up Sunset Inn and see it's on the outside edge of the town that borders Heron Lake.

I open the door, and Cougar sprints in, leaping up on me for a Pup Crunch. Ruby lags behind, limping. My ragged heart is breaking for Ruby, terrified for Haylie, and swollen with anger at a world where evil targets the innocents. And again, knowing that despite everything, it's still possible, I ask for a miracle.

When Ruby finally reaches the door, I help get her settled in her bed, then run to my room to grab Agent Alessio's number off the stack of books on my floor. The books are exactly as I left them. The business card is not. I check my dresser, desk, drawers. Nothing. Until my eyes reach Cougar's bed. Next to his frazzled teddy bear are the remnants of the agent's card. Chewed into oblivion, it's completely useless. No phone number and no wheels. Perfect. I run to Alec's house.

"No way." He shakes his head while slipping on his shoes. "My dad's expecting me at the bakery in twenty minutes. Sorry."

The last thing I want is to get Alec in more trouble, but even that takes a backseat to Haylie's life.

"Come *on*. They could be hurting her right this minute! Can't we just swing by and see if the car is there? That's all. It won't take long. Then you can go straight to the bakery and I'll find a way home." Desperation adds a layer of whine to my words. "Please don't make me ask Kingman. Have a heart, man. Ask your dad."

He grabs his soccer jacket. "He'll kill me."

"Just tell him I need a ride somewhere and you'll be a little late. Tell him it's important. It's the truth." I press my hands together, hoping the gesture will weight my words. "Alec, your dad was in the military. He cares about protecting people. I get it, you guys have your issues, but if he knows it's for Haylie, he'll go for it. *Please*. I'll never ask for anything again."

"I won't even *pretend* to believe that bloody lie." Alec sighs and pulls out his cell.

"Thought it was dead."

"Charged it a bit while you were talking to your buddy out there."

The conversation between Alec and his dad sounds a little sticky, but ends with a "Thanks, sir, I'll get there quick as I can."

"Guess you were right. He said if it might help the kidnapped girl, I should do it. Didn't expect that."

Twenty-three excruciating minutes later we swing into the vacant Sunset Inn parking lot and cruise around the building twice. No cars, no people, no signs of life. The closest building is a boarded-up photo lab that's been closed for years.

Alec puts the car in park as we survey the lot again. "Can't believe the agents aren't here yet."

"I never called. Cougar chewed up the card and I don't have the number."

"You daft idiot! Why didn't you tell me?" He opens his glove compartment and pulls out Smirley's card. "He gave this to me Thursday night. Can't believe you, Nathan. There might be kidnappers here, and no agents are coming? Call the man." He hands me the card, followed by his phone. "Right, then. We're done. I'm not hanging out here a minute longer. There's no bad guys in sight, but if they appear, there's no bobbies or FBI." He puts the car in drive and heads toward the street. "Go on, call. You're doing the right thing, you know."

It's been forty hours since Haylie disappeared. Forty hours and then some. She could easily be in Mexico, Canada, or halfway around the world by now. Or she could be just a few yards away, behind one of those identical doors. We reach the street and I slump into the seat with Smirley's card in my hand.

"Wait." I set the phone and business card in the cupholder between us. Alec stops. A blue minivan pulls into the lot and parks, but it's just a mom who looks like she's yelling at the three kids in the back seat. She shakes her finger at one of them, then turns around and drives away. "Just once more around the lot? Come on."

"Give it up, Nathan!" He's out of patience. Done reasoning. We've done this dance before. "Is this a glory thing, or what? You want to be the big hero? Well, guess what? I've got someplace to be, or did you forget? I know my dad didn't."

"Sorry, dude. I just thought...forget it. Let's go."

He puts the car back in drive and heads onto the street, where we pass a car going into the parking lot—a silver Camry similar to my Dad's, except for a big orange and navy sticker in the shape of a "C" encircling a bear's head.

Chapter 12

Nathan
Still Friday Afternoon

"Stop!"

Alec slams the brakes. I jolt forward, snapping the seatbelt into lock position.

"I saw it. Call Smirley." He nods toward the business card.

"She's in there; let's go!" My mind whirls. It's them. She's here. Gotta save her. "No time for phone calls. Turn around."

But Alec does not turn around, or even slow down. What's he doing? Every second counts.

He stares straight ahead, with a fire in his eyes I've rarely seen. "Don't you get it? I'm not staying!" He hits the gas and my stomach contracts into a ball of molten lead as we continue heading away from Sunset Inn. Away from Haylie.

I stare at Alec in disbelief, wondering how, in an instant, he became a total stranger. Because what he's doing now defies everything I thought I knew about him. "Are you kidding me? What are you doing?" Frustrated, I grab the wheel and we swerve, narrowly missing an oncoming car. He swings his arm, landing a hard punch to my stomach, and I let go and double over.

"You're going to get us killed!" We race past an endless stretch of cornfields. "I want Haylie saved, too, but that's not our job and you've lost your bloody mind! Make the call."

I punch the door, too angry to realize he's probably right. All the stress and fear of these past few days feeds on that anger, building into a hurricane that rages inside me. Getting to that hotel is my only goal. All that matters. Haylie is there and we're much closer than the FBI. I'll do it myself, but I can't do anything from inside this stupid car. "Do what you want. I'm going back. Stop this piece of junk and let me out!"

"There's a car behind me and no shoulder. Like it or not, you'll have to wait."

We continue along the farmland, where there is absolutely nowhere to turn off. Unbelievable. Any other street in this town has houses or strip malls—a million places to stop. But no, we're on the one road that's got nothing. "Just find someplace to turn. Stop somewhere. Anywhere! In the corn. I don't care."

"Are you blind *and* daft? Look at the road. One lane, no shoulder, no side roads or driveways. Just wait a bloomin' minute and I will be happy, thrilled even, to get you out of my car. Oh, excuse me. I mean my *piece of junk*."

"Pull into the field!"

"Shut up!"

My eyes bore holes through the windshield in front of me. We keep going, each minute taking us farther away from Sunset Inn and congealing the air between us. Finally, up ahead there's a side street, but Alec isn't slowing down.

"Up there. Turn there and stop." He ignores me. "Up there, Alec! Slow down and turn!"

"No."

Rage sweeps through me, heating my face, tightening my fists. "I swear I'll smash my fist into your face if you don't turn."

He smirks, which makes me madder, if that's even possible. "Like you could take me. Ha! I'd like to see that."

Under normal circumstances, he'd be right, but at the moment I could take on a sumo wrestler and come out on top. I glance at him, arm muscles tensed under his T-shirt, right hand clenched in anticipation of delivering another punch. He's ready. I'm ready. But what would it accomplish? Us crashing into oncoming traffic? We already came too close. Mad as I am, I've still got a shred of sanity that keeps me from making good on the threat.

"Make the call!" He reaches down to grab the phone but doesn't see what I see. A small, brown spider is crawling onto the screen.

"Alec!" My warning comes too late.

He grabs it and spots the tiny creature, just half an inch from his hand. Eyes widen to saucers.

"Alec. It's okay." I force away the anger, calming my voice, knowing it's the only way to keep us from crashing. "It won't hurt you. I promise." This is our spider routine. He freaks out, I talk calmly 'til he settles down. But I've been through this enough to know it'll get worse before it gets better. Insanely and frantically worse. He throws the phone to the mat beneath his feet. I brace for the scream, but it doesn't come. As Alec repeatedly stomps the phone, the car swerves onto the dirt, then into the middle of the road and back again. He takes a deep breath, then another, and straightens the car.

Hand still trembling, holding the wheel in a white-knuckled grip, he takes a deep breath. "I'm okay," he mumbles to himself. "It's dead and I'm okay." Another deep breath, and another. "It's just a spider. That's all. It's small. I'm much bigger. Big enough to crush it."

It is the fastest arachnophobia recovery I've ever witnessed in my friend, and the first time he's made any effort toward self-composure. I remain silent, letting him calm himself, empower himself. No need to mess with something that's working.

We fly past a side street as he reaches down, picking up the smashed phone and tossing it on my lap, dead and useless. "Look, Nathan. This is real life." Serenity has replaced anger and yelling. Now it's him, trying to calm *me*. "You're not armed and you can't fight off a bunch of criminals. Your head's all bonkers right now."

"*My* head's bonkers? You nearly killed us! And what are you, my therapist? *You're* going to set me straight? That's a laugh." I yell at his profile while his eyes remain glued to the road. "Did you ever stop to think you might single-handedly be responsible for Haylie getting killed? Do you really want a death on your hands?"

Alec winces. I half expect his fist to fly into my face, but he just keeps driving.

"You could've had the FBI on their way sooner if you'd have just called." His words are hushed. Barely audible. A punch would have been less painful.

Straight ahead, an oval price sign slowly revolves over a gas station. "Let me out at that gas station." I'm done yelling, too. I just want out. "Obviously, I'm too far away to help Haylie, so you've accomplished your goal."

Alec nods and slows as we near the gas station. He turns and pulls to an empty area away from the pumps, then parks, continuing to stare straight ahead. "What are you planning to do?"

I open the car door. "I may not have a plan, but one thing's for sure—when I figure one out, it won't involve *you*. In fact, nothing I do from this point on will involve you. Go. Get out of my life." The flash of hurt in his eyes tells me I hit my mark. Again. But a friend is supposed to be there for you, especially in tough times. And he bailed. I get out without saying another word.

"You'll get your wish soon enough, mate." Monotone words. No emotion. No hint of hurt or anger. "It was about to happen anyway." His words confuse me, but I've got immediate issues that overshadow whatever he's talking about. I slam the door hard enough to rattle the car and he drives off.

No plan, no wheels, no phone. No miracles raining down, that's for sure. And no way of getting back to that motel except my feet, which will never get me there fast enough. I don't even have Smirley's card. It must still be sitting on Alec's dashboard. I scan the gas station, my eyes settling on the pay phone. From inside my wallet, a ten and a five stare up at me, but nothing silver. All right, head for the cashier, get change and call someone. But who? As I draw near the building, one name keeps popping into my head. Kingman. Literally the last person on earth I want to call, but he knows how to get to the motel and he'd be talking more than asking questions. Hopefully, we could spend the entire ride talking about his nephew's ponytail or Mrs. Vitalli's dog.

The girl behind the counter is sipping the remnants of her slushy as I walk up. She looks college age, but I'm guessing this could be her top career goal.

"Can I get some change, please?"

"Gotta buy somethin' or wait 'til I open the drawer." Another drag on the chewed-up straw produces the obnoxious sound of moist air struggling to navigate a plastic tube. I'm tempted to tell her the last drop is gone, but she figures it out and stops sucking.

"Can't you just open it? I'm really in a hurry."

She tosses the slushy cup, misses the trashcan, and leaves it on the floor. "Nope."

A rack of candy bars is off to my left, just within reach. I grab one without even looking to see what it is. "Fine, I'll take this."

She nods toward the door. "Hang on. Customer."

"Hey, Billy." She flashes him a smile that never showed up during our brief but irritating conversation.

"Hey, Billie Jo." He offers up a matching smile in return. "Would your beautiful self be willing to break this for me?" He holds up a fifty.

This is a joke, right?

She takes his bill and hands him change. No comment about having to buy something. "How's business? You busy today?"

"Yep. Pretty much."

"Here, too."

I look around at the empty store. Other than an old man pouring powdered creamer into his coffee cup, the aisles are vacant. No one at the pumps, either.

Her customer, the only one that matters, slides the money into his pocket. "Headin' to a fare right now, otherwise I'd love stickin' around a bit."

Her smile fades. "Well, stop back later. I'm here 'til' closin' time."

"I will, gorgeous. That's a promise." He places hand on heart and turns to go. "See ya in a few. And don't forget..."

"Billies are the best." She giggles.

"You got that right."

Please let this be the end of what is possibly the most inane conversation I've ever witnessed, and I'm in high school. I get ready to finally buy the candy bar and get my change, when words jump out at me from the back of Bill's navy blue shirt. "Rocco's Taxi Service, Serving Chicago's Northwest Suburbs."

No way.

"You buyin' that or what?" Billie Jo leans on the counter, her energy completely depleted by the scintillating chat with the taxi driver.

"What? No, never mind."

Her sigh of disgust reaches me just before the door closes. I take off after the driver and catch him as he grabs the car door handle. "Excuse me."

He turns around and faces me full on, a ragged scar marring half his left cheek. Wow, tough business. Suddenly, he seems a whole lot less approachable than he did ten seconds ago, but I'm not here for the companionship.

"Any chance you could drive me somewhere?"

"Yeah kid, I got nothin' else to do."

I pretend not to notice the sarcasm, hoping he'll take me anyway. "Really?"

He shakes his head. "No, not *really*. I'm on my way to pick up a fare."

"Could you just take me to Sunset Inn?"

"Why *would* I?" He opens the door and sits. My best chance is about to slip away and that cannot happen.

"Please." I grab the top of the open car door. "Look, I'm desperate. It's only five minutes away. I swear. I've got $15. It's all yours. Just five minutes away. Please."

"It's closed, ya know. Has been for years."

"I'm aware."

He sighs, rolls his eyes, and points to the back seat.

"Thanks, man." I take a step, stopping as he clears his throat. When I turn to face him, he's holding his palm up. I pull out the bills and place them in his hand.

I haven't been in many taxis, but in my limited experience, they all smell alike. Piney, like Smirley's car, but with the addition of stale perfumes, fast food, sweat, body odor, and vinyl cleaners, which have combined over the years to create a universal taxi scent.

"Do I even *want* to know what you're plannin' on doin' over there?"

"Nope."

"That's what I thought."

Trees whoosh by as he exceeds the speed limit by at least fifteen miles, anxious to pick up his waiting fare. Fine with me. His motive works to my benefit. My eyes start scanning the lot as we pull in. Not sure what I'm looking for, but I don't want to miss anything. There's some signs announcing the demolition, but nothing else worth noting.

Bill slows and flicks his eyes to the rear view. "Where to? Front door?"

"Yeah, that'll do. Thanks." It's around the corner from the room door they entered, so in theory, they won't see me get dropped off. The taxi driver complies, tearing out of the lot the second I'm out.

Once again, I'm on my own without a plan...or an Alec. But I don't need that traitor. I'll figure this out on my own. He's probably at the bakery by now, wiping down scone trays while horrendous things are happening to Haylie. But what does he care? I will never forgive him for this. Never.

I walk along the motel's outside wall behind a line of half-dead trees and bushes that probably looked nice once upon a time. All is quiet and just as empty as before. No one driving by would ever think a girl is being held captive behind one of these doors. Alec was right about one thing: I can't help her from the inside, especially if they're armed, which is likely. But if I can reach the door and listen from the outside, I can gather evidence and testify against them. If they're doing something to Haylie, though, I'm going in. There's no point in considering the consequences.

The only way to continue unnoticed is to use the same plan I used at home when Kingman found me. It failed miserably, but there's no way that's going to happen again. I crawl over dirt, gravel, and years' worth of decomposed leaves and twigs that press into my knees and palms. It takes forever to pass the first two rooms, and there's five more to go. I keep moving forward, creeping slowly to minimize the sound, fiercely motivated by images of Haylie...and those men.

Four more rooms to go. Heart pounding, I inch ahead, jerking when a sharp rock digs into my knee. I pause to let the throbbing subside, then crawl past an anthill and the fragile remains of a bird skeleton. As I stop to remove a thorn from my palm, it strikes me this is the third time I've hidden behind bushes since Haylie disappeared. The veil of night, or even a little cloud cover, would have been a real asset, but the afternoon sun shines like a floodlight on everything around me. Wind would have been nice, too; something to mask my movements and the crunch of leaves, but the air is still. Too still. I freeze and listen, but my heart pounds loud enough to drown out a marching band.

The next door is inches away. I reach my hand forward and freeze as a twig cracks. A leaf crunches. Neither sound came from me. The last thing I want to do is turn my head, but if someone's back there, I need to see. Knowing this might be the last thing I ever do, I wonder if Kingman's nephew will be the one to find my body when construction starts next week. The move does not come easily. With knees and palms in place, I crane my neck. Behind me, a squirrel attacks a patch of dirt with tiny claws, then drops an acorn into its secret hiding place. I exhale, releasing pent up anxiety born of an overactive imagination. The squirrel glances at me and races away, scrambling up a tree. Relieved, I take another breath and face forward, where two fancy brown shoes block my path.

A click is easily discernable above the pounding of my heart. And though I've only heard the sound on crime shows, there's no mistaking the "chkchk" of a gun being cocked. I raise my eyes. Behind the dark and deadly gun barrel, eyes glare at me from the holes of a black ski mask.

"Get up." Calm words seethe with rage. "Now."

I rise.

"Move." He nods toward the door I'd been trying to reach. "Who knows you're here?"

"Nobody."

Shoes crackle over leaves and gravel as we near the door in full view of the parking lot, where no one is there to witness my abduction.

"Lie and you die." He shoves the gun into my back. "Again, who knows you're here?"

"Taxi driver."

"Who else?"

"Nobody. No phone. Couldn't call." I force conviction into my words, knowing he stole my phone, fearing he can read my mind. I glance sideways without turning my head. No sign of the FBI. No sign of anyone. Too late to wish I'd listened to Alec, or to finally realize everything he said made sense. That calling Smirley was the way to go. That letting the professionals handle it would have resulted in Haylie getting saved, instead of both of us captive. Or worse. No point wishing I'd made productive choices instead of stupid ones...but I do.

We reach the door and he tells me to stop, then bangs twice. "Open up! Put your mask on."

"Why are you back?" Sounds of movement come from inside, followed by footsteps. The door cracks open. "I thought you were..." A huge man fills the opening in the doorway. "What? Who's this? What's going on?"

"Forgot my wallet. Came back and found this one crawling behind the bushes."

As the man in the room steps back, I'm shoved from behind and stumble inside. His large meaty hand grabs my wrist as the door slams shut and I'm left with no plan, no way of showing the FBI which room they're in, and nothing but a burning desire to rescue Haylie. Bound and gagged, she sits inches away from me. I was right. I *knew* she was here. But it's a hollow victory, void of triumph or satisfaction. Haylie is no closer to getting rescued than she was before I entered this room, and I'm powerless to prevent whatever happens next.

Chapter 13

Nathan
Friday afternoon

"Just perfect!" The huge bearded guy who answered the door yells at the man with the gun. A large vein throbs in his neck, just below the bottom edge of the mask. "This is your fault, Steve! *Your* fault! 'No one will get hurt,' you said. 'Easy money,' you said. Now what? What are we supposed to do with *him*?"

Behind him, a guy in jeans and a black T-shirt sits on a stained mattress, leaning back against a pillow. He is also masked, but says nothing.

I'd like to suggest they let us both go, but I'm guessing they don't want my input. Thoughts ricochet off my brain as I consider ways to lunge for Steve, grab Haylie, and escape. None of those scenarios end well for us, especially with two other guys in the room.

"Seriously? You just said my name out loud? It didn't dawn on you that this one can hear? That maybe we need to stay as anonymous as possible?" Steve's volume increases with each question. "Nice going, *Rob*! Calm down and think before you speak. Right now, less said, the better."

"Like it matters at this point," he mumbles.

Desperate for Haylie to know I'm here, I take advantage of their argument, hoping it distracts them from what I'm about to do. I grab her blindfold and tug. Her eyes squint, open, then open wider, staring at me with disbelief. What has she been through? If any of them touched her, I swear I'll...

That cold, steel barrel presses into my temple. "Another move like that and you're history. Am I clear?"

"Crystal." I don't regret the move. She knows she's got an ally in the room. It's the best I can do.

Rob tugs Haylie's blindfold back into place, then grabs a bag of plastic ties off the dresser. He pulls some out as Steve points the gun to a spare chair in the corner, then to me. "Grab that," he tells the guy in the chair. "Get him secured. I don't have time for this."

"My shift is done." Jeans doesn't move. "I was just leavin'."

"One more hour," Steve says. "Extra pay."

"Triple, or forget it."

"Fine, just do it. I should have been on my way by now."

Triple pay must be just the motivator Jeans needs. He grabs the chair and shoves me into it, then helps Rob wind those ties around my feet and wrists. But from the looks of Rob, being a bad guy doesn't come naturally to him. His bright red neck shimmers with perspiration. Hands fumble and shake as he works the ties. And that vein is still pulsating like it's going to burst. Rob's heading for a meltdown. Breathing in the stale air of this condemned motel room probably isn't helping him, either.

"Let's just abort this whole thing," he says. "I want out. Tell them we can't get it."

"Too late for that. Ten minutes ago, they sent me this." Steve pulls out his phone and shows it to Rob.

"Oh, no! No, no. They took a kid? Who is he?"

"My boy. He's six. So I'm telling you right now, we're

going to get it and deliver it to them, and nothing, *absolutely nothing*, is going to stand in my way."

"Okay, okay. I get it." Rob slides the chair so it's back to back with Haylie's while Steve stands by the curtains, keeping his gun pointed in my general direction.

Another kidnapping. A child. My stomach drops at the thought of that scared little boy held captive. Bad enough he's got Steve for a dad, now he's abducted, too. These men have let greed infiltrate their hearts, poison their minds, convince them that attaining some material thing is worth whatever it takes. Whoever it hurts. And they're too blind to see the damage it's done to their souls.

There has be some way out of this, something brilliant that just hasn't come to me yet. If it were a movie, the actor playing me would disclose a critical piece of information. A secret document hidden in my gym locker. Something. And as we all went to get it, Haylie and I would miraculously escape and the cops would be waiting nearby to arrest the bad guys. But I already know how the reality would play out. They'd keep Haylie here and shoot me when they saw the contents of my gym locker: smelly shoes, a towel, goggles, and a quarter I found on a bench last Monday.

"Wait!" I hunt for what to say next, when there's absolutely nothing to offer them. Zero bargaining tools. Still, I need to try. "Let us go. We won't tell a soul about you." I blurt it out, knowing they won't buy it. Knowing it's meaningless. "We won't tell anyone where you are. It will be a lot easier for you to get away if you don't have us to drag around."

Steve laughs. Kind of like the Joker, with just the right touch of insanity to make it disturbing. "Shut up, kid."

But I can't shut up, because my voice is all I've got right now. "How about a trade then? Me for Haylie."

"Shut up!" Steve waves his gun at me again as if I didn't notice it was there. "Do you need convincing?" He takes a few steps over the grungy beige carpet, stopping about two feet away and holding the gun at face level. *My* face level.

Something about that gleaming hunk of metal pointed at my head fosters a cooperative spirit on my part. I stay silent. Any wrong move could put Haylie in more danger. And remove my head from my body.

"Gag him. I gotta go." Steve extends his arm, the gun now just inches from my face. I stare down the barrel and my brain melts. With the pressure of just one finger, he could detonate my brains, turning them into oatmeal. One finger, one squeeze, and I'm nothing more than a memory. A picture on the mantle.

And then what? Heaven. Amazing place, from what I hear, but I'd like to put that off for a while. I thought Ruby would be the one to get there first. Regret washes over me in waves. She should have been there already; out of pain, running and playing and being endlessly happy. And it should have been me taking her to the vet for the last time, holding her as she left this world. But I kept hanging on, and now I'm here and may never get to say goodbye.

My eyes can't stop fixating on the gun. Heat consumes me. The gag is blocking all the air. Can't breathe, but I need to stay conscious. Need to save Haylie. I breathe in through my nose, then do it again. Here we are, at the mercy of these morons. It wasn't supposed to go this way. I was supposed to be a hero, not a victim. Steve waves the gun and sneers. A drop of sweat trickles down the side of my face as I wonder how painful it is to get your head blown off. Will I feel my brain exploding into little bits of mush? Or will it be like one second I'm here, and then...not?

"Make sure they're tight." Steve points to my wrist ties with his gun, then turns to Rob. "I'll call you after I talk to them. Relax, okay? We got this. I'm outta here." He peers through the curtains, then leaves.

Everything inside me is running like an overheated

racecar.

Giant Rob crouches to tighten the plastic around my ankles, then stands. "Let's find something to use as a blindfold so we can take these things off." He slides his hands under the ski mask and stretches it out to let in some air. "I can't stand this thing. Can hardly breathe."

"Chill," Jeans says. "Whatever you guys are up to, I'm guessin' you'll be rollin' in dough pretty soon. That should help you breathe just fine."

"Maybe. I don't like this, though. Not what I expected." He turns to me. "What's wrong, kid? Nervous?"

I could ask him the same question. He's not like the others. Maybe we have more in common than being extremely unhappy about our current situation. Maybe we both made really bad decisions that landed us in this motel room, even if we're on opposite sides of the equation.

"See, this is what happens when you mess with someone else's business," he says. "You should have just stayed out of it. Believe me, I don't like you being here, either."

No point in responding. If they were going to kill us, they wouldn't bother with ties and masks. For now, we live. And just maybe we'll survive this whole thing and I'll get my second chance with Alec. That fight in the car was stupid. If we can get past all that, I can talk to him about other things. See if I can get him to come clean about his Saturday afternoon disappearances. Maybe I can even find a way to convince him to get counseling for the burden, whatever it is, that he's been carrying around like an anchor all these years. That should have happened long ago. I just thought we had time.

Until death stared me down with its round black eye.

Fear rages through me, wraps around me. Mocks me. But I have to break free from it. I look at Haylie, sitting there like a broken angel. For her, I will clear my head. She deserves that much from me, little as it is.

Rob rubs his forehead as he and the other guy look for something to use as a blindfold. "We got any aspirin in this place? My head's killin me."

Jeans rolls his eyes. "Seriously? I think we got other priorities."

"Sorry. A little new in the role of criminal mastermind."

Jeans laughs. "You may be a crackerjack scientist, but criminal mastermind? You guys are a disaster. When this hour is up, I'm collectin' my pay. I'm done. I'm used to workin' with pros. You guys ain't no pros." He searches through empty dresser drawers and under the bed without finding anything to use as a blindfold. "And no, there ain't no aspirin. There's two bottles of water, chips, and a stale cinnamon roll."

Maybe I can use Rob's headache to my advantage. The info gets filed away in a corner of my brain – the area I'm storing ammo for breaking us out of here.

"What about antacids, we got those? I could really use a couple."

Jeans guy shakes his head. "Unbelievable," he mumbles.

While they look around the room, I push my wrists and ankles against the ties. Just a test, one I expect to fail. Rob did his job well. I won't be making a move unless the chair comes with me. I'm about as helpful to Haylie as a teddy bear, and not nearly as comforting.

Jeans sees me struggling against the ties and walks over, raising his hand to Haylie's face. The plastic ties cut my wrist as I struggle to prevent whatever he's planning, but he only glares at me and puts his hand back down. It was just a message. A warning. I take a breath. Fear and panic want to wreak havoc in my head, but once I give in, there's no chance of us making it out of here alive. Another breath. *Assess the situation.* During the minute or so when I could see Haylie, she looked like they hadn't messed with her. Her clothes are intact. No visible bruises.

Some unrecognizable song emanates from Rob's pocket. He pulls out a phone.

"Yeah." He listens. "I have *no idea* how he found us." He turns to me. "Hey kid, how'd you find us?"

Jeans pulls my gag off. "Don't even *think* about yelling."

My mind goes blank. I don't want to put Burnout Neighbor Guy or Mr. Kingman in danger, but I have to say *something*.

"Answer him!" Jeans raises his hand to Haylie's face again.

"Uh. Ummm. I found a Sunset Inn matchbook. In the alley. Thought it might be a clue, so I checked it out." It sounds so ridiculous, I half expect them to punch me unconscious for being the world's worst liar.

Instead, Rob turns to Jeans. "You drop a matchbook from the motel?"

Jeans scratches his neck. "I don't know. Could have, I guess, when we grabbed the girl. I took one when we were settin' up the room." He tugs my gag back into place.

They bought it. I don't know why, but no point in questioning a gift like that.

"The kid found a motel matchbook," Rob says into the phone. He pauses to listen. "Nah, he was behind the girl's house. Our guy here says he might have dropped it. Anyway, better the kid found it and not the feds." He listens again. "Okay. Call later. I want to know what they said." Another pause. "Yeah, yeah. And bring some aspirin. Steve? You still there?" Rob looks at his phone and slips it back into his pocket.

"You guys got a Plan B?" Jeans gives up looking for a blindfold and sits back on the bed, where he opens a bag of chips and starts munching.

Rob sighs and gestures toward Haylie. "She *was* the Plan B. Never thought we'd actually need her. We figured it would be much easier to get it. The thing we're trying to get."

What's *it*? What on earth could they need to get that would involve Haylie? They have to want something from her parents. What does a vet have that they'd want? Something animal related, or medical. Maybe that animal tranquilizer stuff some people use to hallucinate. Maybe they're ransoming Haylie for the drugs and selling them. And they picked Wild Things because drugs for gorillas and lions are way more powerful than what a regular vet would have.

Rob looks over at me and Haylie, then back at Jeans. "I've said too much already. Forgot we're not just dealing with the deaf girl anymore."

Rob continues looking for a blindfold. He tries a towel, but even the cheap, thin terrycloth is too thick to tie behind my head. He walks behind me. Bedcovers swoosh before his footsteps clomp toward me again. As he comes back into view, a pillow dangles from his hand.

My heart picks up speed…again. Suffocation. I'd rather be shot than spend the last three minutes of my life struggling for air. A weird, guttural sound emerges through my gag as I whip my head from side to side.

"Relax, kid." He slips off the pillow case and tosses the pillow on the floor, where it lands with a poof against the desk leg. He stretches it out to wrap around my eyes. In less than a minute I will be without my vision, voice, or mobility. If I'm going to make a move, it better be while I still have sight.

Bent in half and attached to the chair, I shift to my feet and leap, ramming headfirst into the soft, unsuspecting middle of Rob's stomach. The unexpected move knocks the breath out of him. He crumples. He tries attacking me, but I keep my back to him, swinging the chair legs in his direction. I swing away, mind whirling with potential escape strategies. Breaking a window with a chair leg might attract someone's attention, but there's no way to get the chair high enough to reach the window. I continue swinging back and forth frantically until it smacks the door, but the adrenaline rush keeps me going. *Smack!* It connects with the window frame, inches below the glass, sending a vibration through my body. I nearly fall, but catch myself and swing again, dislodging the curtain enough to let a streak of sunlight in. *Smack!* Wooden legs crash into Rob's knee. He yells out a few choice words, graphically describing what he's going to do to me. It doesn't sound pleasant.

He crouches, face contorted in pain, then nods toward Haylie. "No, don't hurt her. We can't hurt her."

I spin around to see Jeans' fingers around the soft, fair skin of Haylie's throat. Like a baby chick in a lion's jaws, Haylie could get the life crushed out of her and never see it coming.

"Settle down, Rambo, or the girl dies."

Wooden legs clunk against the floor as I clumsily try to sit, but getting back in that position is far more challenging than getting up. The chair tilts over and I crash, lying sideways next to the desk like an overturned Teenage Mutant Ninja Turtle. Some hero.

Muffled sounds emerge from just outside the window, but there's no time to wonder about it because Rob's big black shoes fill my carpet level view.

"Idiot!" He screams at me. You've made everything worse!" Maybe it's the pain shooting from his knee, or his headache, or the stress of waiting for Steve. Maybe he's just a vicious jerk, though he doesn't want Haylie hurt. Whatever the reason, his foot swings back. My eyes squeeze shut. I turn my face upward, knowing that foot is torpedoing toward me with the force of a wrecking ball. A white light explosion bursts through my head before everything fades to black.

Chapter 14

Air whooshes around me as small earthquake tremors rumble the floor beneath my feet. Something is going on and all I can do is sit here like a rock. Useless. Unable to help the person who risked his life to help *me*. How he got here and how he's involved remains a mystery, but he's in danger now, that much I know. Whispers echo in my head. *There's nothing you can do, Haylie. Nathan's going to die, and there's nothing you can do. You're useless. Useless. His death will shroud you for eternity.*

I am painfully familiar with these demonic voices. Wordlessly, their whispers drift on silken threads that weave through my fears and insecurities. Dragging me into the bleak depths of hopelessness. Chipping away at my faith so I'll forget the immense power of the one who loves me unconditionally. What's faith, then, if it's only acknowledged when all is well? Do I abandon it now, when I need it most? Evil surrounds me, making its presence blatantly obvious in the men who took me, in the hate and terror rising up in me, filling my heart so there's no room for hope and courage. A formidable mission, because that's the room where faith's power comes alive. But in this moment, when hope and courage seem to be a galaxy away, it would be so easy to believe all is lost.

So easy...and so pointless. I squeeze my eyes closed behind the blindfold, forcing myself to remember God did not create me to be weak and fearful. My power, my strength, comes from Him. And if ever there was a time to tap into that, it's now.

Please, God, help Nathan.

My neck muscles ache from the last time I tried to maneuver this stupid blindfold, but I have to see what's happening. The floor vibrations tell me someone is stomping or falling as the air continues to move in tiny breezes. I mimic the move I made yesterday, raising one shoulder and tilting my head to rub against it, hoping the men are distracted by whatever's going on and won't notice me. The side of the blindfold scooches up just enough to provide a slit of vision, but that's all I need.

Grizzly is bent down, grabbing his knee, his face scrunched in pain while Nathan stands bent at an awkward position, tied to the chair. He yells something at Nathan, then turns toward me. I fear he'll notice the slight angle of the blindfold, but he looks past me, over me, then jerks up his arm, palm facing me in the stop position. His head shakes rapidly in a desperate plea to prevent something. The gesture is oddly protective. Whatever's happening behind me, he wants it to stop.

Relief washes over me. Maybe we're safe, or at least relatively safe. If he doesn't want me hurt, it's possible he doesn't want Nathan hurt, either. For reasons my brain can't ponder in the midst of this insanity, maybe we're more valuable to them alive. There's a shred of comfort in the thought, until warm fingers wrap around my neck. Grizzly faces me, looking directly at my face this time.

Nathan does the same, his eyes wide and wild as he screams, "No!" Grizzly speaks to him again. The slight pressure around my throat remains, but does not increase. This is it then. This is it. My pulse races. Death by strangulation. I always thought drowning would be horrible, but this...this is worse. I wait. Hold my breath. My poor parents - all three of them. If only I'd had more time with my father. More time to get to know him and consider his brokenness. To forgive. He's been trying so hard. And Ben, crazy and sweet and innocent. This is going to wreck him. I should've played Scrabble with him. What a stupid thing to think about. Everything in me tenses, waiting for those hands to cut off my airway. Waiting for death; trying to focus on what's beyond. And still, the hands do not squeeze.

Nathan struggles to get the chair back in place. No easy task...I would know. He comes down at an angle and one leg hits the floor and slips. His crash landing leaves him lying sideways, his head next to a pillow as though someone placed it there, anticipating his fall. Instantly, the hands release my throat. He's okay. I'm okay. We survived.

But Grizzly's face tells me there's more to come. With his face twisted in pain, his neck tomato red, and eyes blazing hatred, he stares at Nathan. My hands grip the chair, holding on tight because only something horrible can result from that much anger. I hold my breath as an ogre-sized shoe swings back, then rockets forward toward Nathan's head. My would-be hero anticipates the blow with eyes closed tight. I want to do the same, but can't tear my eye away from the impending savagery.

No!

Silent screams blast through my head. My throat rumbles with a sound I know without hearing. It rises from the darkest place inside my soul. The cavern where terror is born. Grizzly's shoe whacks Nathan's head and his eyes open wide, then close again. His body slumps. There's no signs of life in the boy who risked everything for me. My body slumps too, not knowing if he's unconscious or dead. Fearing the worst. Feeling like there is nothing left of me. No reason to survive this ordeal. Oh, Nathan. I watch for a twitch, a breath, anything, but tears obscure my vision, dripping from the opening in the blindfold. Nathan blurs. *Please, God.* It's the only prayer I can manage. No other words will come. *Please, God.*

I tilt my head to see Grizzly, picturing him behind bars for the rest of his life. He reaches for the curtain, which isn't hanging the way it's been when I've had my blindfold off for meal breaks. It's slightly askew, allowing a fissure of sunlight to streak in. He starts to fix it, then stops and stares outside, grabbing his head as he turns toward Jeans. They both gesture wildly. I stare, focusing on that white patch of beard. I scan my memories, determined to find that beard. That face. School, Wild Things, neighbors, people I see when I'm running along the lake. Each face falls away without any connection to my captor...until one hovers in my head.

Take Your Child to Work Day. Eighth grade. Mom showed me around ZetaLab, explaining some of the instruments and projects, and introducing me to her coworkers. "You have to meet Rob," she'd said. "He'll be back in a second."

I picture the watch. *To Rob with love, Mary.*

I have to recall everything about meeting Rob. There's got to be something of value in the memory. We'd waited by his desk, where a half-eaten sub sandwich sat in foil next to a food-smeared newspaper. Only it wasn't a regular newspaper. It had horse photos and lists of races. It had that logo – the same one on his jacket. Mom said it was a racetrack form, but the concern in her eyes prompted me to ask if that was bad. "Not always," she said, "but I'm worried about him. Some people take it too far." I knew she was thinking about my father, so I didn't ask anything more.

When Rob returned he scribbled a note. "Hi, Haylie, I've heard so much about you." He smiled with shiny white teeth gleaming like porcelain soldiers amidst the thick, graying beard. A beard with a white patch where there was no pigmentation.

Grizzly is Rob.

Now I know who did this, how he knows me, and that it's connected to ZetaLab. But why...and for what? I don't even care. I just want him in jail. Forever. I want him to pay for what he did to Nathan, but the truth is, there's no sentence that could ever atone for what he did.

My eye returns to Nathan. The men ignore his lifeless body, but in this dreary, hopeless room, where my heart lies in shatters on the floor, he is all that matters. Live, Nathan. Please, live. *Please, God. Not this. I can't.* My eye scans him from head to foot, aching for a sign of life. Longing to see the slightest movement as I linger on his face, his chest. Did it move? Is he breathing? It's too hard to see him clearly enough to tell. A slight tilt of my head brings his hands into view. Plastic ties fasten his wrists to the chair. This is no way to die. Tied up. Brutalized by wretched, heartless, disgusting, repugnant excuses for human beings.

Secured to that chair, he lies still as death. Until...his thumb moves. I think. Did I see it twitch, ever so slightly? I crane my neck forward, drawing every ounce of energy to my eye, straining to see that thumb move again. It's all I want. A sign. Something to tell me he's still in there.

His thumb bends. His fingers curl. My gaze shifts to his face, where brown eyes squint at me like he's trying to focus. *Lie still, Nathan, let them think you're dead. Don't make a sound.* If only he could hear my thoughts, but I know it's impossible. Still...hope prompts me to try. The men don't pay attention; they just keep talking to each other and peeking outside. Hearing isn't usually something I wish for, but right now, I'd take it. Knowing what these guys are saying would be amazing. Not that it would change our circumstances, but as I continue watching their faces, I see all I need to know. They're upset. Afraid. Jeans steps toward me and my breath comes short. Now what is he planning to do? I'm so tired of wondering, of being afraid, being at their mercy, worrying about all the people I love because *they* chose to trespass on my life. I've had it! A hot, misty haze fills my head. But it is not fear. It is anger.

Red hot and boiling over.

I've had it with their intimidation, these ties, the brutality. They have no right. I look at Nathan lying half-dead on the floor. Even now, he may not survive. The force of that kick likely caused a brain bleed and who knows what else. Without immediate treatment, he could still die. They will pay for this. If not in this world, then the next. Personally, I hope it's in this one first—the sooner, the better. Jeans guy pivots and returns to the window.

I close my eyes and breathe deep, wracking my brain for a plan. *Come on, Haylie. God didn't give you a high IQ for nothing. Use it.* Slowly, hardly moving at all, I tilt my head, searching the room, their faces, their gestures in the tiny patches my blindfold opening allows. The tension that's been my constant companion since arriving here is heightened by a new force: panic. I can see it in the quick, jerky movements of my captors, and the drop of sweat sliding down Rob's neck. I can feel its static charge in the air.

Lowering my chin provides a view of the floor. An empty hamburger bag lies crumpled not far from Nathan. Dirty, worn carpet. Shoes. The garbage can holds a racetrack form like the one I saw years ago on Rob's desk. More carpet, candy wrapper, the bottom of the door.

Snake.

Am I losing my mind? The black, wiry thing slinks into the room from beneath the door. No eyes or tongue. Faceless. I freeze, giving it all my attention. Looks like a computer cable, only stiffer. It pauses, turns right, then left, as if looking around, and eases back under the door. There and gone in seconds. It had to be a camera, just like on the cop shows. But one question burns in my head. Are the people behind the scope good guys, or more of what I've got right here?

My gaze shifts back to the men, who apparently didn't notice the snaky spy cam. I can't help wondering if panic is making me crazy enough to think I saw something that was never really there. It all happened so fast, and the tension has been constant. Maybe this whole situation is plunging me into insanity.

Glass shards explode from the window, clawing my skin and confirming someone's out there. A small round object bounces twice on the floor. It stops about three feet from my chair. I jerk my head toward the men, who stare like wide-eyed deer at the mystery object. Only it's not a mystery at all. Because nothing else looks like a grenade.

The world erupts. Harsh light flashes like the flames of hell. I am blinded in my left eye. Waves of air accost me, but they are not like wind. They are not like anything I've ever felt. My body shakes right through to my soul. I can't see. Can't think. Can't move. A gray haze thickens the air, saturated with the scent of fireworks.

More vibrations. Heavy. Fresh, cool air gusts into the room. As my vision slowly returns, the motel door comes into view, but it's lying on the floor. Sunlight pours through the opening, streaming through the haze as if in a dream. Or a nightmare. Immense black boots move toward me, while others move toward the men. Terror rips through me as my consciousness falls away. I try to hold on, stay awake. Stay alive. But it's getting so hard. Where's Nathan? I raise my chin toward the sunlit opening...and wish I hadn't.

Monsters bolt through the door. Monsters with armored bodies, round black helmets and very, very big guns.

Two of them grab my chair, whisking me outside without bothering to untie me. I breathe in through my nose, grateful for the fresh air and dreading what comes next. Because every time I think it can't get any worse, the devil swoops in to prove me wrong.

Chapter 15

Nathan
Friday night

Doctor Sanford towers over my ER bed, clipboard in hand. "You have a minor concussion, Nathan, along with some swelling. You're a lucky young man, though; that's for certain."

There are many words I could use to describe my current situation. *Humiliating* and *painful* come to mind. Even *pathetic* might make the list. *Lucky* is not even a blip on the radar.

"Am I?"

"Absolutely. The agents said there was a pillow between your head and the desk. Without it, you may have been getting spoon fed the rest of your life. I'd say you got yourself a miracle today."

The pillow. The amazing, life-saving pillow that, for a moment, I thought would be my undoing. The instrument of my death.

Thank You.

We are encircled by a blue curtain, with just enough room for my bed, a couple of chairs, a tray table and a few feet of standing room. Dr. Sanford glances at the heart monitor, then back to me.

"I can guarantee you'll have a nasty headache the rest of the night. Probably tomorrow, too. The nurse will give you something now for the pain, and I'll write you a prescription for the next two days. After that, plain old ibuprofen." He tucks his pen into his shirt pocket and begins to walk away. "Call me if it doesn't subside. And by all means, get some rest."

Rest. There is nothing I'd rather do. Haylie's safe, and for once I really get that old phrase about having the world on your shoulders, because it just lifted off and left me feeling weightless. My parents thank the doctor, but before he leaves our cubicle, he turns to me. "A couple of federal agents have been waiting to talk to you. I'll let them know you're ready."

I'm so not ready.

A nurse comes breezing in with Agent Alessio and Smirley on her tail as my parents shuffle aside to make room. She hands me two green pills and a glass of water. "These will make you feel better, hon, but it will take about fifteen minutes. Best for you to sleep soon as you're done with the agents. Hopefully, by tomorrow you'll be back in your own bed." She turns toward Smirley. "I'll let your wife's nurse know you're here. She wasn't expecting you 'til later."

"Thanks. Please tell her I can only visit for a minute. Still on duty. Then I'll come back later."

"Will do." She smiles and disappears through the curtain, leaving me to wonder what that was all about. Not that I'd ask.

Smirley glares at me from behind my parents. No doubt my unsolicited involvement didn't endear me to him.

Agent Alessio's eyes look like they'd welcome about a week's worth of sleep. And a good vacation. The kind with a lounge chair facing the ocean, where your only responsibilities are soaking up the sun and breathing in the scent of coconut oil.

"How are you feeling, Nathan?" Thin creases etch her forehead. I tell her I'm fine and wait to see if my "buddy" sounds concerned, but he stands silent and poker faced.

"How's Haylie?"

"She'll be fine. We brought her straight here from the motel. The doctors checked her out and sent her home. No injuries. She was quite worried about you, though. We were impressed with the details she remembered, which will help us a lot." She settles into the chair next to my bed. "I'm going to jump right in, because you'll be getting groggy soon. We need to clarify a few things."

"Okay."

"You got information from Haylie's neighbor and ran with it instead of calling us. Why?"

Dad leans forward, eyebrows merging into one. His glare proclaims his displeasure with that little stunt. "Nathan? Are you *loco*? You had their card. The phone number. All you had to do was call."

"Well, I was going to, but..." And then I freeze, unable to come up with anything that sounds remotely reasonable. The problem is, everyone is staring at me like I'm on stage, and it's getting more uncomfortable with each silent second. Words start pouring out, but my explanation sounds lame, even to me. I tell them I wanted to figure out the meaning of "sunset" so I could call with more information, and that Cougar chewed up the card with the phone number. Next up is the bad guy's car pulling into the lot, and me telling Alec to stop and Alec being a dope. And that his phone "accidentally" got damaged. I definitely didn't mention that, in hindsight, Alec wasn't the dope.

"Everything happened so fast." Hopefully, she buys that line and doesn't push for details. "All I could think about was saving Haylie. That's all, just saving Haylie." But I know the truth, and it's more selfish than honorable. I wanted to be the one to save her. Not them.

Smirley shakes his head, pursing his sneery lips. "Well

thanks to the *FBI and SWAT team*, Haylie is safe, but you certainly complicated the situation. Your antics could have resulted in both your deaths. You know that, right?"

All I know is that my head is pounding harder now, and this isn't what I need. If he's got questions, I wish he'd just ask them and hit the road.

"Sorry." I try to telepathically tell Alessio the apology was meant only for her.

Agent Alessio looks at Smirley and rubs her forehead. "It's all right, Nathan. What's done is done and I'm glad you and Haylie are okay and we caught these guys. Truth is, you did play a key role in finding them. Your method was a little unconventional, but somehow it all came together in the end."

Smirley responds with a "hmph" while Mom looks at me and shakes her head. This must have been a nightmare for her.

"Thanks." I hope she can tell I'm being sincere. Her words mean a lot to me, especially after listening to Smirley. "And again, sorry for not calling."

"Now tell me, what did they say? I need to know everything you heard. Imagine yourself there from the first moment you encountered them. Close your eyes, Nathan. It will help you visualize and remember. Give me a play-by-play." Alessio is ready with a pen and notebook, while Smirley records me on his phone. I close my eyes and picture crawling behind the bushes, Steve catching me, and that part with someone taking his son. Everything that was said or done until the moment that shoe collided with my head. Naturally I missed the best part—the whole SWAT rescue thing.

Alessio nods and stops writing. "Good job. Can you think of anything else?"

I shake my head and pain wraps around my brain like a boa constrictor. Note to self, no more head shaking ever, ever again.

"Do you have any questions?"

Only about a million. "What happened after I went in? How did you guys know where to go? What was happening?"

"Ah, the rescue. I thought you'd want to hear about that." She rubs her eyes, running her fingers through her hair. "After your friend Alec called…"

I lean forward. "You mean, from the bakery?"

"No, from a gas station down the road. He went back to get you, but you were gone. He said you two had an argument, which I notice you didn't mention. He was at the motel when we got there and showed us which door the kidnappers went into. I couldn't get that kid to leave. Agent Smirley argued with him, but he wouldn't budge from the motel entrance. Kept saying he's not leaving his best mate, or something like that. In the end, Smirley let it go since Alec wasn't in the kidnappers' line of sight."

So Alec came back for me. *And* he stood up to Smirley. Even after what I said to him. I feel the corner of my lips turning up and guilt enveloping my soul.

"Thank goodness his father showed up and finally got him in the car. They still stuck around, but at least they were out of the way."

Interesting.

Alessio says she called the SWAT team, and just before they arrived, she and Smirley heard yelling and banging coming from Room 156.

"It was perfect," she says. "Just the sign we needed. SWAT slid a fiber optic camera under the door. That's when we saw Haylie tied up and you still as death on the floor. We had to act fast. They tossed a concussion grenade through the window."

"This is what they call a flash-bang, yes?" Dad loves this stuff. He finally got a chance to use a term from one of his crime shows. It's not often "flash-bang" pops up in conversations.

"Yes."

Mom gasps, hand flying to her chest like her heart just

stopped. "This could have killed them!"

"No, ma'am. Concussion grenades were developed for situations like this. It creates an ear-shattering blast and blinding light that stuns people long enough for us to burst in. It actually sends out shock waves." She whooshes her hands to mimic the air waves. "Haylie couldn't hear it, of course, but she could feel it and see some of the light through her blindfold. We got the kidnappers cuffed before they knew what hit them."

This is going to sound corny, but it needs to be said. "Thanks for saving my life. Haylie's life too."

Before Alessio can reply, Smirley takes a step toward me. "Yeah, well it wouldn't have been necessary if you had talked to me in the Summers' backyard."

Maybe I would have if he wasn't such a jerk, but I keep that to myself. It seems like too much effort now that the meds are kicking in. The pain fades to a dull ache as my eyelids strain to stay open.

Mom strokes my hair, which wouldn't be so bad if there weren't two feds in the room. "You should sleep, *mijo*. You need to heal."

Sleep. My eyes ache to close and shut away the world. My body is becoming one with this mattress. But no way. Not until I find out how a simple pizza date led to a kidnapping, interrogations, and terrorists. "I need the story, Mom. More than anything. Then I'll rest like crazy. Promise."

"All right, but you better keep that promise. I want you back home and well again."

I look at Agent Alessio, waiting for the answer to the question that's been burning in me since Haylie disappeared.

"I can't give you all the details, but here's the short version." Alessio explains that Mrs. Summers had been working with a coworker to develop a way to convert radioactive waste into plutonium. "This is a big deal, you see, because plutonium can be used to make nuclear weapons. Her partner told his friend Steve about it. Both men, for different reasons, were in situations where they desperately needed a lot of money." She pulls a water bottle from her coat pocket and takes a sip. "It was supposed to be for the U.S. military, but Agent Smirley found out these men had a foreign contact willing to pay millions." She glances at Smirley, who nods his agreement. Funny how his face kinda softens whenever Alessio talks to him. No sneer, no glare. Almost human.

She explains that Mrs. Summers suspected something was shady. She didn't know what it was but knew her coworker had gotten into heavy debt with gambling and feared he might be desperate enough to do something criminal. She was right, but without proof, or any validation for her suspicion, she couldn't accuse him of anything."

I fight to stay awake, wanting to hear every word, but as the meds diminish the pain, they deplete my energy.

"Rob filled us in on everything. He's been very cooperative. He said Steve found buyers and they made a plan to sell the formula once they found a solution to the last glitch. But Mrs. Summers followed her instincts and kept the completed formula on her laptop, with a printed copy at a friend's house. Very smart woman." Alessio clears her throat, then gulps more water, looking like she hasn't slept in days. "The other guys each had *parts* of the formula, but only *she* had the finished version. She called in sick the next day, trying to buy time to figure out how to prove her suspicions."

The weary agent shakes her head. "These guys were on edge, Nathan. They figured she knew they were up to something and couldn't take the chance of her telling anyone. Their deadline with the terrorists was approaching. Rob, in particular, was in over his head. He and Mrs. Summers had been work friends for years. They'd talk about their kids, so he knew things about Haylie. Since they didn't get the formula the easy way,

Steve convinced Rob to use that information to kidnap Haylie, promising no harm would come to her. Rob told us he hated the plan but went along with it. That's what desperation does to a person. He had no other way of paying his debt and was terrified of the consequences."

My thoughts zero in on the conversation in Mrs. Summers' kitchen. She'd said she worked with "really nice" people. "So what happened after she left?"

"Steve and Rob hired professionals to pull off the kidnapping and kept one of them on to watch Haylie during the day. This way, they could both go to their jobs without looking suspicious. Mrs. Summers had already told them Haylie was dating a swimmer named Nathan, so it wasn't tough for them to find you. They followed you and Alec to the soccer field and found a little *gift*: your cell phone sitting on the front seat of Alec's car."

"Told you I didn't send that message." I direct the comment to Smirley, who ignores me.

Despite the pain medicine, my stomach crunches in on itself. It was *me*. My fault. If I hadn't left that stupid phone on the seat...

"They figured if they took Haylie, Mrs. Summers would do anything to get her back," Alessio says.

Smirley touches her shoulder. "I can finish up." He steps closer to the bed; the glare is gone from his eyes. Probably because he's in my parents' line of sight. "They hired guys to grab her from the alley and bring her to Sunset. After Steve caught you snooping around, he left to meet the foreign buyer and beg for a little more time."

Mom shakes her head, covers her face with her hands. "This is all so crazy."

"Yes, ma'am," Alessio says. "It surely is. And that's where you entered the picture, Nathan. They didn't count on some teenager foiling their plan."

"Thank you, agents. We are most grateful for everything." Mom stands up, her signal that it's time to go. But Agent Alessio asks her to "please sit."

Her mouth becomes a thin line. "Nathan." The pause that follows pulsates with something dark. "There's more." She turns toward my parents. "Steve is still out there, angry and desperate. The terrorists are holding his little boy until he comes through with the formula. Haylie and her family are in a secure location, but Steve is smart as well as dangerous. We think he may try to get it. She doesn't have the laptop, but he knows that formula is in her head."

Mom's face goes from Peruvian tan to Wonder Bread white as Alessio continues. "We're doing everything we can to get him in custody and get his son back home. Poor kid."

Mom grabs my hand, her ebony eyes shimmering with frightened tears. "You do not leave the house, *mijo*. *Comprendes?* Not even for one minute. Do not go in the yard, do not even go by the door."

"He's not after me. He's after Haylie's mom. He's got no reason to hurt me, Mom. He wants that formula."

"I do not care what he wants or does not want. Stay close to home until he is caught. Promise me."

Her hand is trembling. There is only one thing to do. I nod and promise, knowing I am lying right to my mother's face. Steve is out there. Steve is going after Haylie's family, which means he might try to hurt Haylie. And that's not going to happen.

No matter what I have to do to prevent it.

Chapter 16

Haylie
Saturday afternoon

I tilt my face to the sun, letting its beautiful brilliance warm my face as we head down the dirt path leading to the tiger enclosures. We pass the twins, Sasha and Misha, sleeping on a sunlit rock, their golden fur gleaming in the light. I turn toward Agent Smirley. "Poor things spent years caged up in some rich guy's private zoo."

He shakes his head. "That should be illegal." His signing is quick and flawless, making me wonder if he grew up with someone who's deaf.

Next up is Fang, his sleek muscles rippling as he strides across a low hanging tree branch. I tell Agent Smirley that a year ago, he was nearly too fragile to walk. Neglected by owners who bought him as a cute cub and were completely unprepared to care for a full-grown tiger. I blow a kiss to Fang and keep walking, anxious to check on Mika before visiting Imani.

"Just a little farther." I point to Mika's enclosure ahead. "She came to us when she was four months old and I was ten. We kind of grew up together. Her owner got her as a baby and was making a bunch of money letting people pose with her. That's very stressful for tigers. Most animals, actually. We never do that here. We don't breed them or train them or let anyone touch them, other than a few staff members. We just try to give them a good life after other people have abused them."

"This is a great place," Smirley signs. "I'm impressed with all the space they have to roam around."

We reach Mika's area and I tell him I just need a few minutes, then we'll head over to the other side of the sanctuary where the huge gorilla building and outdoor yard are located.

"Whatever you want to do is fine, as long as we leave in an hour." He looks at my beautiful Mika, three hundred pounds of power and grace, and I see the look of awe I've seen on so many others who come to visit our tigers. "This place is amazing," he signs. "I'd stay if I could, but I have to get to the hospital. Sorry."

Such a nice guy, but there's a sadness in his eyes and I consider asking about the hospital visit but decide to let it go. Maybe on the walk back to the car. "Thanks for explaining everything to us. It's still hard to believe my mom created something terrorists would want. Or that her own coworker would kidnap me. He seemed so nice when I met him."

"He probably wasn't a bad guy, but desperation changes people." Agent Smirley must have seen so much of this over the years. People leading normal lives, then something happens to set them off course – a tragedy, a bad decision - and they cruise downhill into darkness. "His gambling addiction destroyed everything."

Something in his eyes tells me he knows this isn't the first time I've suffered the consequences of someone's gambling addiction. I seem to be a popular form of collateral damage.

"Smart man. Good job. No priors. Now he faces years in prison." He shakes his head. "He cooperated fully, though. That will help. And you were a big help, too, with all the information you gave us. Now we just need to get

Steve. I won't rest until that guy's in custody."

I can't help wondering what will happen to Jeans. He couldn't be much older than me. Mid to late twenties, maybe. Agent Smirley said he had no interest in anything but getting paid to do the job. It's what he does. You need something illegal done, he's the guy. Not anymore, though. What a waste of a life.

Dad waits by Mika's gate, smiling as we approach and shaking hands with Agent Smirley.

"I heard you leave at five this morning," I say. "Why so early?"

"Too much time away from our furry friends the past few days. There was a lot of catching up to do." Dad unlocks Mika's gate and the door swings open. "I've been focused on someone other than our shelter residents."

I step inside and Agent Smirley stays on the path. "I'll be right here." He smiles, and I know he's wishing we'd invite him to come inside, but that's not a good idea for him *or* Mika.

Our magnificent Bengal leaps off a tree stump and strolls over to us, nudging me with her head until I almost fall over. I laugh, grateful to be part of this animal world, loving the feel of her fur on my face, and wishing she'd been born wild. My arms wrap around her, feeling the strength of her powerful neck and shoulders beneath the orange and black striped fur. She should be roaming the deserts and grasslands of India, chasing down antelope and water buffalo. She should be free, but like Imani, she lacks the survival skills.

Dad and I check Mika's tooth and see she's nearly recovered from the infection. Her amber eyes are clear and bright, and her appetite is back to normal. With another hug and a promise to return soon, I leave her and rejoin my temporary bodyguard.

Together we enter the primates' indoor enclosure and breathe in the acrid, musty scent of urine, feces, food and a hint of chemical cleaner. It assaults my senses, but also welcomes me like the salty sea air to a sailor. Agent Smirley scrunches up his face, but his expression doesn't tarnish my excitement. As we near the meeting spot, he gently touches my arm.

"There's only half an hour left. I just wanted to remind you. I apologize for the time limit, but unfortunately, it's necessary."

"I understand. Thanks for letting me do this. It means the world to me." I speak truth. It would have made me insane not to come here today, to be stuck at home. Or what we're calling "home" these days. It's more like a lesser form of captivity.

I ache for life to return to normal, or whatever the new normal looks like. There's no going back to seeing the world from the same perspective as I did a week ago. A new wariness pervades me now – a wisp of darkness that casts suspicion on everyone I encounter. Is Steve watching me get into my car? Is the woman walking behind me involved with the kidnapping? Is our FBI apartment really a secure location, or did someone hide a camera in there before we moved in?

It's not surprising, considering all that's happened. The surprising part - the saving grace - is how the paranoia is balanced by the joy I feel from people and experiences that, until now, were relatively unremarkable. Eating ice cream with my family, running with the breeze in my face, texting my friends. Knowing I *have* friends and realizing some people don't. And...eating peanut butter cups.

We move toward the indoor jungle, where the primal scents of earth and leaves blend with the fragrant jungle flowers: pink and white impala lilies, the lavender-hued verbenas, and my favorite, Bird of Paradise, with their vibrant orange blooms resembling the head of a fancy crane. The botanist who chose them didn't sign, but that didn't stop twelve-year-old me from plying her with a million questions while she worked. And it didn't stop her from answering every one. I gaze through the menagerie of exotic flowers and gnarly vines dangling and tangling, weaving around trees and surrounding the pool and waterfall – a masterpiece we never could have accomplished without an amazing and unexpected donation from an anonymous celebrity. My heart thanks that person every time I enter. We continue to walk along the empty tourist path. An hour from now, people of all ages will walk along this trail, breathe in the moist jungle air, and be amazed at the beauty and power of our four lowland mountain gorillas. I peer through the branches, vines and flowers until my eyes land on the only one that matters in this moment.

Imani eats alone at the base of a Marula tree. She stops in mid-apple, eyeing me through a thick plexiglass wall. The apple falls, rolling beneath a giant fern. She freezes, locking her eyes on mine, then explodes around the enclosure, leaping, running, bouncing. Mouth wide open, her primeval shrieks are lost on my dysfunctional eardrum, but somehow I feel they are loud and long, hailing from the depths of the African lowland forest. She swings from rope to rope, banging joyfully on trees and walls, then heads toward me as Dad and I laugh at her toddler-like behavior. Oh, how I've missed my overgrown, hairy friend! But she's never approached me so fast and with such wild abandon.

An unfamiliar fear creeps into me as she draws near. I step back, muscles tensing. Imani jumps down, landing with the force of a cement block dropped from an airplane. The vibrations reach me from five feet away. Still locked on my eyes, she stops, moving only her hands.

Girl afraid?

Dad looks from Imani to me. *"Are you?"*

I shake my head. It was just a moment, that's all. A fragment of anxiety remaining from days in darkness, wondering what might happen next. Looking into the deadly black hole of a gun barrel. Jumping each time I was touched. It was just that; nothing more. But to Imani, it was everything. She knows my heart.

No. Girl loves Imani. Come here. I wave her over, a sign she knows well.

Open door. Brown eyes gaze at me, shadowed by her protruding brow. Wide nostrils breathe in my scent with a quiver. She opens her mouth to let me know she's happy to see me, but not enough to reveal teeth that can rip through tree bark.

Dad releases the bolt on the keeper's gate—sturdy steel bars separating the plexiglass – then unlocks the cabinet housing the tranquilizer gun. He pulls it from the rack for a quick inspection to make sure it's ready to fire.

As if.

Imani walks gingerly toward me, thick, bushy arms striding forward, eyes asking, "Where have you been? Why did you leave me?" Too many words that she can't sign...but she doesn't have to. She pauses to sit, then opens her arms. I go to her, instantly enveloped by the musty hairiness I know and love. I am safe here in these shaggy gorilla arms—safe from evil, greedy men. Safe from the fears that tormented me for three days. My pent-up emotions flow out, soaking Imani's chest. She hugs me tighter, shrouding me in her fur, but careful not to crush her fragile human girl. At last the tears subside and I ease myself from the warmth of her body.

Imani touches her index finger tips to the outside corners of her eyes, then points to me. *Girl sad?*

I can't lie to my beast. *Yes. Girl missed Imani.*

A black, leathery hand reaches out to envelop mine. We sit, side by side, speaking in silence. No words, no signs. In my head, I tell her about the bad men, how happy I am to be home, that I was worried about her and now I'm so afraid for Mom. I tell her Steve is still out there, scheming, plotting, posing certain danger. And if anything happens to Mom...

My body shudders in an unvoiced sob. Imani responds

by leaning over to wrap her arm around me, though her comforting gesture invokes a tinge of guilt. She doesn't know I never liked primates until she came along. I hung around for the tigers and jaguars: Mika, Fang, Sasha and the rest. Each one a primal masterpiece of grace, power, and beauty, so different from the gorillas, with their maniacal grins and nauseating odor.

I pull away just enough to look at my beast, huge, confident, comfortable and safe in her makeshift jungle, and remember the little creature that came to us orphaned and afraid, needing a friend and comforter. It was Dad's idea to bring me into the picture. All I wanted to do was see her, our newest primate resident, then go back to my cool cats. But she reached out with her little wrinkled fingers and grabbed my hand. And with it, my heart.

I guess it's true that God works in mysterious ways. Nothing about this relationship makes sense. Everything about us is different. And yet, we connect in ways that science can't explain, and that the world may not understand. We were given the gift of each other, and that's all we need to know.

Chapter 17

Nathan
Saturday, Early Evening

"And with us now is Nathan Boliva, the Beethoven High senior who played a key role in Haylie Summers' rescue."

Year after year I've sat in this worn corner of the couch watching the news, and now *I am* the news. Unbelievable. Mom tosses the pillows off the couch and settles down with a plate of almond shortbread cookies and a blueberry scone, courtesy of Alec's dad. I reach over and grab one of the cookies as she's setting the plate on a tray table. In the kitchen, chocolate-filled sponge cake and almond puff pastries take up the middle shelf of the fridge. Apparently that ex-spy English baker plans to mend my concussion with sweets.

Mom points to the television as she's done several times during the past two days. "Look, Nathan, there you are!"

My face fills the screen. It's so weird to watch myself on TV. Ever since freshman year, reporter Miya Turner has revealed the details on high school shootings, bank robberies, weather disasters and murders. She is my daily companion, though we'd never met until the interview. She tells me what's happening in the world, but there are some people you're just never supposed to meet in the flesh. They are designed to appear only on television and computer screens, talking about other people's lives. Other people's catastrophes. I lean forward as my unsolicited moment of fame continues.

"Tell us, Nathan, what made you go to the Sunset Inn, and what happened once you got there?"

The television me recites my rehearsed version of the story, carefully wording it the way Agent Alessio told me. Cutaway shots of Miya show her nodding with a camera-worthy expression of compassion and fascination, then it's back to me recanting the SWAT rescue. Next, Miya introduces Haylie, whose soft, sweet face graces the screen, along with her mom who's there to translate. Haylie thanks the police and FBI for all their work. And right there, in front of thousands of viewers, she thanks God for watching over us.

"And what about Nathan Boliva? Is there anything you'd like to say to him?"

Mrs. Summers signs the question to Haylie, who smiles with a hint of pink rising in her cheeks. "Nathan was very brave," she signs. "I can't believe he took that risk for me. I just want to thank him. He's a pretty amazing guy."

Mom gives me an exaggerated wink. "Pretty amazing, eh *mijo*? I like this girl." She gets up from the couch, taking her empty coffee mug into the kitchen. Haylie's face disappears from the screen, replaced by reporter Richard Sanchez standing amidst a bunch of scraggly looking cats.

"Coming up next, police find twenty-six abandoned cats in a one-bedroom apartment." Like Miya, he is adept at putting on a camera face, but something in his eyes says he would rather have covered the kidnapping story.

I click off the television and stare at the empty screen. Forty-eight hours of house arrest, and I'm not even the bad guy. Two days of being stuck inside, texting, reading, playing with Cougar, sitting with Ruby, and programming my new phone. At least Alec came by yesterday. A little awkward for a few minutes there—a first for us. But after some arm punches and name-calling, it was business as usual. Too bad about his cell, though. Can't believe he smashed it. Bad break, but at least he gets to go to school. I'd give anything to be on that bus tomorrow – a pathetic commentary on my current situation.

Mom heads upstairs to shower, reminding me that Dad will be home in an hour or so. "Don't open the door for anyone," she tells me for the twentieth time, "and I mean anyone, Nathan. *Entiendes?* Unless it is Alec or one of the agents. Remember what Agent Alessio said—someone can just *pretend* to be an agent. So if it's not one we know, do not open."

Yeah, yeah, yeah. My life is in danger. I get it. "What if it's the president? Or Abuela Dora? Or a millionaire handing out money?"

"That's enough, Mr. Smart Pants. You know what I mean." The bathroom door clicks, followed by the whoosh of water. I examine my silent surroundings, waiting for an exciting idea to enter my brain.

Waiting.

And still waiting.

It's hard to believe there are people who are afraid to leave their houses. Staying inside makes me "bonkers," as Alec would say. At least Haylie and I are getting to know each other a lot better through texting. I replay her videos of Imani and the tigers whenever I'm bored – a recurring status, and one I find myself in yet again. Everyone's at swim practice or work. Sean's got play rehearsal and Alec's at soccer, otherwise he'd be here. No interest in more Internet searches. I already looked up the fire science classes I'll be taking next year, who teaches them, and which books I need. It pains me to know I'm caught up on what's going on in the world, *and* what all the celebrities are up to. And I don't even care about the latter.

Peering through the slits in the front window blinds offers nothing but the unchanging view of my street. Harder to see now that it's dark, but no doubt, still the same. Headlights pierce the darkness and stop under the streetlight in front of Alec's house. A Mustang. Looks like it might be red, but I can't tell for sure. I feel like Kingman, spying through the blinds, but boredom and curiosity win out. A figure emerges from the house. I would know which Channing that is from a mile away on the blackest night. I click off the living room light for a clearer look.

Cat traipses down the stairs, that awesome mane blowing behind her, in jeans that fit like they're painted on. As she walks to the car, a guy gets out and walks around to open her door. A small gesture, but it makes me happy that she's with someone who would do that. Part of me always considered her off limits to the rest of the world. But that part of me has grown up, and I just want her to be happy. Anyway, I've got Haylie now. I hope. Sweet, beautiful, brilliant, fiery Haylie.

They drive off, leaving nothing else worth spying on out there. Even Kingman probably stops surveying the neighborhood by this time. I try in vain, for the billionth time, to think of ways to find Steve or protect Haylie. If I could find him and his little posse the first time around, why am I drawing a blank now when it's life and death?

Staying inside is making me crazy. It's too hard to think inside these walls that mock my inability to save the day. I peer out the window again, where the night air beckons me and the lake calls my name. A few minutes out there will do me good. I grab my jacket, then stop to kiss Ruby on the head. Next to her, loyal Cougar keeps her company with eyes that see the pain she's enduring. He doesn't even follow me to the door.

Outside, the scent of freedom floats on the night breeze. I breathe it in before heading for the rocks. Man, this feels good. Phone in hand, in case Haylie texts again,

I sit on my favorite boulder, watching the lake shimmer under a band of moonlight. A black periscope pops up in the middle, looks right and left, then dives back under. A lone cormorant. He should have flown south by now with the rest. I wonder what he sees down there in that black water. Pretty soon he'll have to go too, along with the ducks, cranes and herons. If I had wings, I'd definitely make headway to a place with sun, sand, and water that stretches to the horizon.

Alec would likely do the same. Seems like sometimes he's already in another place —one that's heavily fortressed. When I attempt to invade, he just laughs and says he's thinking about a girl or some upcoming soccer game. He is lying. It's something he needs to do. It's something I need to accept because that's what best friends do. But I can't help wishing there was a way to tear down that wall, because I'm almost certain that behind it, I would find Jenna. Maybe then I could help Alec free himself from whatever is keeping his heart in chains.

Fish flop out on the water. I can't see them, but the splashes are a familiar sound. The three-quarter moon is still bright enough to beam its glow onto the water. Haylie will like this if we ever have a chance go sit here together. Or even have that elusive date. But my thoughts are intercepted by a menacing aura; a discord in the atmosphere that causes my hands to involuntarily grip the granite beneath me. My fingertips feel the grit of each tiny crevice in the rock. The earth holds its breath...and so do I. Even the geese are silent. A ghostly chill creeps over my little section of shore as I stare at a fixed spot on the black water. My brain commands my legs to run inside, but my legs ignore that order. Now there's only one thing I know for sure.

I am not alone.

A step, then another. I tell myself it's a skunk or possum. Maybe even a coyote. Considering the alternative, I'd be okay with that. A shoe scrapes against the rocks. None of my preferred options wear shoes.

"It's about time you came outside."

The familiar voice generates a serpent of fear that slithers up my back. It wraps around my neck, choking me as I wonder how I could possibly have been so stupid.

"I was growing tired of waiting."

"What do you want, Steve?" My voice seems to emerge from far away.

"One simple answer, then I'll be on my way. Where's your girlfriend's family hiding out?"

"I don't know. She didn't tell me."

"Wrong answer. I'm out of time and patience. I need the location now. Right now."

"And I don't have it. They were told not to tell anyone."

"Last chance. Where are they? You're going to hate the consequences if I don't get an answer."

For the second time in my life, I hear the gut-wrenching click of his gun.

"I *don't* know. I can't give you an answer I don't have." He wouldn't get it either way, but there's no point in saying it.

He sighs. "Didn't want to do this, but I'm out of options. Sorry about your shoulder."

"What are you talking--"

Pain explodes through my shoulder, knocking me off my boulder and onto the smaller rocks that line the shore. The sickly flow of warmth streams from my shoulder onto my chest. Honking, quacking, wings beating water. Yelling. Feet running on gravel. Agonizing pain shoots through my shoulder and arm, pervading my entire body.

A voice emerges in the distance. "What's going on out there? Get out of my backyard! Off my grass! I'm calling the police!"

Footsteps thud across the lawn. I squeeze my hand and feel the phone. Wet, sticky...but still there.

Oh God, give me this before I go. Please, just give me this.

I try to raise the phone to my face, but the message gets lost between my brain and hand. Footsteps again, this time crunching over rocks and getting louder. A beam of light slices through the darkness. He's back. I'm dead for sure.

"Who's there? Is someone out there?"

The familiar gravelly voice greets me like an angel song.

It's me, Mr. Kingman. Nathan. I need help! The words do not come out as words at all, just a low groan that sounds more animal than human. The beam of light hits my feet and swoops to my face.

"Nathan? Oh no, no! Oh, my goodness! So much blood! Nathan, can you hear me?" He kneels next to me, face close to mine. "I'm going to help you. Just stay right there. I'm going for help."

I gather up every ounce of power within me, which is almost none, and move my phone hand a few inches toward Kingman, then press my thumb to unlock it.

"Call."

"Eh? What now?" He leans closer, ear practically touching my mouth.

"Call."

I try to fight the blackness closing in, but I'm losing the battle. Little time left. I tap Agent Alessio's name, then lose the ability to move. "Ear."

"Hear what? You hear something?"

I'm going to die before Kingman gets this. "My *ear*."

Amazingly, and I mean *absolutely amazingly*, he places the phone by my bloody ear without asking why or what or anything. Two rings lead to the voice I need most right now.

"Alessio."

My shoulder's on fire. My back is soaked with the life flowing out of me. I try to get the words out, but they won't come.

"Nathan?" Agent Alessio's voice floats on the air from a hundred miles away. "You okay? Nathan?"

Come on, Nathan, you can do this. "He's here." Each word thrusts daggers into my head. "Warn Haylie."

And suddenly there is no noise, no pain. No Kingman or beam of light. There is nothing.

Chapter 18

Haylie
Saturday, Early Evening

Scrabble pieces crisscross the board, forming six words including Dad's 30-pointer for "quest," which elicited a "woo-hoo" *and* a fist pump. At least he spared us the victory dance, but only because it's still early in the game. When we're done, I'll tell them they don't have to entertain me every minute of this exile to a government-owned apartment. The endless line-up of board games, movies, and even a ceramics craft with my uncrafty mom is starting to wear on me. I survey my letters as Ben sits next to me on the floor offering unsolicited tips and getting mad when I ignore them.

"It's not fair." He flips through his Pokemon cards and complains for the third time since we started the game. "You guys are mean."

"Enough, Benjamin." Dad victory smile fades away. "You've been part of every game today. You can sit this one out." He stops for a spoonful of pistachio ice cream, then surveys the board.

"But I'm a great speller."

"Scrabble is not for the faint of heart in this family." Dad licks his spoon, not wanting to miss a single drop of his favorite flavor. "Your mother is ruthless and your sister eats Scrabble pieces for breakfast."

He's not wrong. I'll play any other game with Ben, even let him win on occasion, but Scrabble brings out the dragon in me. Same for my two middle-aged competitors. Little Ben, with his limited vocabulary and belief that Scrabble is just about spelling words, wouldn't know what hit him. Still, a tinge of guilt ripples through me. "After I have a little alone time, we'll do something, okay? You choose."

"You're just saying that 'cause you didn't let me hang out when your other dad came to visit. Even though I --"

"Ben!" Mom's look silences him. "I'm not going to explain this to you again."

His gaze drops to the carpet. "I know, I know. They're still getting to know each other and all that."

Mom places her letters on the board, spelling "anoxia" for 23 points. We all know better than to question it, but she knows we want to. "Absence of oxygen."

Anoxia. Pretty much sums up how I felt when I saw my father walking toward our car that first time. Not so much last month, though, when we met at a vegetarian café. His choice. I touch the silver heart necklace that arrived the night I got kidnapped; a purchase that probably cost him a day's pay at the box factory. But he bought it, anyway. For me.

Mom nudges me. "Your turn." Her competitive spirit is exceeded only by her lack of patience.

Words stare at me from the board, but instead of focusing on ways to beat them, I let my thoughts linger on this morning, when my father took a bus and walked two miles to see me, then hugged me so tight I could have passed out from anoxia. And I didn't even mind.

"Thank God you are safe. I was so worried." His signing was slow, but it was obvious he'd been practicing. "I had to see you. I hate myself for all the years I have missed. But I don't regret signing away my rights as your father."

Anoxia. That's what happened when he said those words this morning. I should be looking for a word to spell, but it is my father's words that fill my head, drawing me away from the game.

"I didn't deserve you. I wanted you to have a wonderful life, but I was too weak and damaged to provide it. And broke. So broke. When I met Russell, I could see how much he loved you and your mom. I could see goodness in him and knew he would provide for you and protect you. Give you the good life that I could not. Does that make sense?"

For so many years, I'd walked the hazy line between hating him and aching for his return. How many times had I wished he was living a miserable life? How dare he just give me away! I put up my boxing gloves, ready to punch away the love and logic in his explanation, but there was no fighting it. He did what he did out of love. It was a screwed-up kind of love from a messed-up guy, but it gave me an amazing life with my mom and stepdad. When I looked at him this morning and saw his pain, his regret, and the grievous toll of his mistakes, I felt nothing but compassion.

"Nothing good comes from hate. Even self-hate." I signed slowly, watching his eyes to make sure he understood. "It eats you up and prevents you from moving forward."

He smiled, his eyes glassy. "How did you get so smart?" He kissed my forehead, and we made plans for him to visit Wild Things the following week. Mom even agreed to pick him up. Forgiveness was softening her heart, too.

The sweet memory of this morning spreads warmth through my heart, but it's still fragile. Healing, but marred by the scars that remain from him leaving me. Still, there was something about that kiss.

"Come on, Haylie. I have a game to win." Mom grins at her little joke.

Her comment whisks me back to the here and now. I stare at my letters, seeing if there's a high-scoring spot to place "wrist," but Mom jumps up to answer the phone. Back home, I would have known the phone was ringing. I miss having those flashing lights. I miss everything about our house.

Mom's face tenses. Wrinkles line her forehead. She glances at me, then down, in a futile effort to hide the bad news coming through the receiver.

"What's going on?"

Dad shakes his head. "I don't know. It sounds like she's talking to one of the agents. I think someone is hurt. Let's just wait and see."

Not Nathan. Please not Nathan. Anoxia stares at me from the board. Engulfs me. Suffocates me. I watch Mom put her hand to her mouth. Jaw tight. I cannot survive much more of this waiting. We stare at her, all three frozen in place, until she finally hangs up and faces us.

"Nathan's been shot," Mom signs. "But he's okay."

My heart falls out of my chest. Mom blurs.

"Steve shot him in the shoulder. No one knows why. Maybe it was revenge for Nathan messing up his plan. He asked Nathan for our location."

"He doesn't know." I'd wanted to tell him, but the agents said not to, so I complied.

"I told them that. Nathan is in surgery right now."

"I want to go. I want to be there when he wakes up."

"You can't. Maybe tomorrow, but tonight we have to stay in. They have someone stationed outside."

"I don't care. I'm going." I stand, determined to be by his bedside when Nathan opens his eyes.

"I'm sorry, honey, there's just no way. Too dangerous. And if you go tomorrow, you'll have an FBI escort. It's the only way." She walks over and joins Dad on the couch. "Even if you snuck out, the agents would stop you. You need to wait until morning. Then you can go. Promise."

It never ends. Even getting rescued didn't end it. It's

worse than ever. Four days ago, Nathan's life was school, swimming, hanging out with friends, playing with his dogs. My biggest issue was whether to trust my bio father enough to let him back into my life. And in an instant, our worlds imploded because these horrible people ruined our lives. And for what? So they could steal a formula that other demons could use to ruin even more lives.

I try to hold on to my faith, to gain strength from the only one who can provide it, but I stop short, choosing hate instead. Hate for the bad guys, for guns, for chemical formulas with the potential to destroy. It consumes me in a white-hot fury that blazes through my body. I flip the board, its little wooden squares scattering across the floor, and run to my room and slam the door. Only it's not my room at all. And this isn't my life at all. As I crumble to the floor in sobs, all I can picture is Nathan lying on a surgical table, being sliced open, with the very real possibility that when he awakens, he will no longer have use of his arm.

Chapter 19

Nathan
Saturday Night

I am floating beyond space and time, engulfed in a fog of tranquility. Opaque shadows swirl through the place where thoughts and memories once existed. They allow no sense of movement, no fear, no joy, no feeling. Nothing matters. I just *am*. Maybe it's a good place, but I don't know for sure and don't care. There is comfort in the silence.

Something breaks into my world—something small and warm and wet. It runs down my arm. Fingers gently stroke my head. Once, twice. A small, painful sound breaks the silence. Tearful words drift into my head. *"Por favor, Dios..."* but I can't make out the rest, though I know that accent well. "Please, God." It's all she says. I am torn between wanting to remain within the comfort of my peaceful world and allowing myself to be pulled toward the sound of that broken heart. A heart that tugs at my own with increasing force. No, let me stay. Let me float aimlessly. Let me exist in this hazy wasteland between life and death.

The fingers softly rub my arm. *"Por favor, mijo. Te amo mucho"* Son. She called me her son. I love you too, Mom.

Her soft voice continues, just above a whisper. "Open your eyes, Nathan. Do it for me." The fingers glide down my arm to hold my hand.

Somehow, I know this simple action will pull me from my safe harbor into a turbulent sea. I just want to stay and float forever.

She gently squeezes my arm. More warm drops fall onto it. Another hand now, this one heavier, rests on my shoulder. A deeper voice with a matching accent enters my world. "Give him time, Cristina. He'll be okay, won't you, *mijo*?" My father's voice cracks a little on the "son." He says nothing more.

A tender voice tells me what I must do. Tender, yet powerful. Soft, but clearer than church bells. Its message is unmistakable. My hand obeys, gently squeezing hers.

I hear a gasp. Her hand tightens around mine. "Nathan?"

"What, Cristina?" My father's voice. "What is it?"

The next hour is a blur of tears and hugs and phone calls. I find out Haylie is all right, but Steve is still at large. Doctors come in and out. Blood tests. IV checks. Nurses asking, "Can you feel this? Can you move that?" They tell me the bullet missed the subclavian artery and just skimmed the brachial plexus.

"That's great news in terms of your recovery," Dr. Cho says. "The plexus is a large nerve bundle that controls your arm function. Suffice to say, another quarter inch over and your problems would have been much more severe. Possibly permanent. Still, there will be months of recovery and physical therapy. You're young and strong, though. You should pull through just fine."

He bends to examine the five stitches on the left side of my forehead. "Heads and rocks are never a good combination. At least you fell from a short distance." He stands and turns toward my dad. "There are too many people in the waiting room, Mr. Boliva. Old and young, toddlers, grandparents, the works. Plus, an English family that won't leave, and some reporters. Can you please go talk to them?"

I can just see it—a room full of my emotional Peruvian relatives and my stoic English neighbors. Pass the *aji* and scones and let's have a party.

"*Si*, I will talk to them," Dad says, "but my parents will not leave without seeing their grandson. They are stubborn people, Doctor. If you can just give them five minutes with Nathan, they will comply with your request."

I jump in before the doctor can reply. "Alec too. Please. Five minutes."

The doctor isn't happy with the plan but says it's better than the present craziness. He accompanies Dad, who heads out to give the family an update and ask them to go home. When Dad returns, *Abuela* Dora and *Abuelo* Cristobal are with him. Alec trails close behind. He hangs out by the window, politely giving my abuelos time with me.

Their wrinkled brows make my heart wince. Abuela Dora's hand flies to her mouth at the sight of my bandages. She dabs her glassy eyes with a tissue, then showers my face with kisses. Abuelo Cristobal holds my arm with both hands, like it might fall off any minute. I assure them, in Spanish, that I am feeling fine and will see them again tomorrow. Mom and Dad leave to walk them out.

Alec is next. Jaws tight, eyes intense, he's in worse shape than the night we hid in the dark by Haylie's house. I imagine myself in his shoes, seeing him in this sterile room, shoulder wrapped, knowing how easily that bullet could have ended everything. If I almost lost my best friend to a bullet...well, I get it, that's all. He needs to know I'll be all right.

"Oh, man," I groan. "They sent the wrong Channing. I wanted the hot one."

Silence, until the pain slowly melts from his eyes and a

hint of that Alec grin emerges. "Got your wish, mate. Here I am, but you're really not my type. If it makes you feel any better, Cat's all worried about you. Said I should give you a hug from her."

"Please don't."

"I assume just knowing she said it is good enough."

"Works for me."

He holds a familiar blue paper bag imprinted with English Bakery but doesn't hand it over. Instead, he shakes his head and settles into the chair that Mom occupied moments ago. "How's the pain?"

"Still under the influence, so nothin' yet. They say it's coming, though, so there's that to look forward to."

"Can't decide whether to call you loco, barmy, or just plain stupid."

"I know, I know."

"Why would you go outside?" He opens a box of chocolates on my nightstand and helps himself to one.

"He wasn't after me."

"And yet, here you are. Or at least, what's left of you."

"I *know*."

He finally plops the bag on my lap. "From Dad."

"Chocolate hazelnut cookies?"

"Biscuits, Nathan. Biscuits. Speak English."

"*You* speak English."

And so it goes.

Alec reaches over to steal one of my cookies. I pull the bag away, glare at him, then open it so he can take one. He takes two. "Well as a matter of fact, the *reporters* liked my English just fine. Talked to three of 'em in the waiting room—Channel 5, Channel 9 and The Daily Heron." He brushes crumbs off his jeans. "That newspaper girl...wow. I'm going to marry her."

Tapping draws our attention to the window. A light rain pelts the glass. "Nice. I get the pain, you get the fame. Why doesn't that surprise me?"

"Relax, mate. They'll be all over you as soon as the doc

lets them. At the moment, me and your parents were the closest they could get."

"We have a lot to talk about, Alec."

"Just chill," he says. "Everything's good now. We'll talk when you're better."

Yeah. We will.

Commotion in the hallway draws our eyes to the door. My aunt and uncle wave and call out, "Love you, Nathan" before the doctor guides them away. Guess they missed Dad's announcement.

He shakes his head. "The whole world has gone barmy lately. You need anything, Nathan? Anything at all, you name it."

Here we go. "Tell me where you go on Saturdays."

Alec focuses on the machine humming next to my bed. "No fair. We had a deal, and now you're breaking it just because you're in the hospital."

"I'd really like to know. No judging."

"How about I think about it?"

Not what I wanted, but I'll take it. "That'll work."

My parents walk in with their Styrofoam coffee cups, Mom grimacing as she takes a sip. Apparently, it doesn't come within miles of her coffee standards.

"All right, guys." Dad walks over and stands by Alec. "I think that's enough for today. We promised the doctor five minutes, remember? Alec, tell your dad thanks for the biscuits. If Nathan is too weak and fragile to eat them, I will make sure they find a good home."

Alec gives me a gentle nudge to my good arm. "Gotta go, anyway."

As he leaves, the doctor returns with papers for Mom and Dad. He drones on about what I can and can't do for the next few days before finally leaving the three of us alone.

A triple knock turns all our eyes toward the open door. Alessio and Smirley saunter in, greeting Mom and Dad before Agent Alessio drags a chair over from the other side of the room and plops down. "Déjà vu. No more hospitals after this, okay?"

"That's my intent."

"Can you handle a few questions?"

"Sure."

"What did Steve say?"

"He wanted to know where Haylie's family was staying. I told him I didn't know, which is true. I wouldn't have told him if I did."

"Anything else?" She pulls a notepad and pen out of her jacket pocket.

"No. He said 'Sorry about your shoulder,' then he shot me. That's the whole thing."

Mom looks into my face and stands up. "Please, agents, my Nathan has been through so much. If you would make this brief, I would be most grateful."

Smirley nods. "Yes, ma'am. We're about done."

Oh sure, you're nice to *her*.

"Okay, son, let's finish up here." Alessio flips her notepad to a blank page. "He shot you, then what?"

It only takes seconds to recap the scene. I tell them about Kingman, my unlikely hero. Finding me bloody on the shore had to be a leap or two above watching the grass grow. He'll definitely have plenty to talk about with Mrs. Vitalli.

A nurse stops in and taps the tube, then injects something into it. "This will prevent pain, now that the anesthesia is starting to wear off, but it'll also make you tired." She pivots to face my suited guests. "Best to wrap up this visit in the next few minutes."

"We're finished. Thank you." Alessio rises from the chair.

Smirley breaks his gaze away from the window, gracing us once again with his attention.

The agents go first, followed by my parents, who are driving my grandparents home, then coming back. Silence pervades the room for the first time since I opened my eyes. It frees my mind to contemplate the enormity of what happened. I journey back to the beginning of this rocky adventure. It hits me that, at every fork in the road, I took the wrong path. Knowingly. Which led to coming face to face with a gun, that, despite my worst fears, never blew out my brains. My head got kicked but was protected by a randomly placed pillow. And a bullet to my shoulder missed a major artery instead of blasting through it. Theoretically, I should still be able to join the college swim team next year.

And against all odds, Haylie's still alive.

The meds flow through my body, relaxing muscles, sinking me into the heavenly wonder of the hospital mattress. And as I drift away, I smile, thinking how funny it is that we beg for miracles and don't even recognize them when they're raining down in torrents.

Chapter 20

Haylie
Sunday Morning

This is a nightmare. It's been a lifetime since last night's call from Agent Alessio. A lifetime of worrying, praying, and waiting for morning visiting hours. What must Nathan be thinking? From the moment he asked me out, his life's been a mess. Questioned like a criminal, held at gunpoint, kicked in the head, now *this*. He could have died. The phrase firmly planted itself in my brain last night, taking root and sprouting. Nathan could have died. *Again*. And even though he didn't, he won't be swimming anytime soon. And the pain. I can't even imagine the agony of a thirty-eight caliber bullet ripping through flesh and muscle.

Meeting me has ruined his life, and we never even got to have that pizza.

We pull into the hospital parking lot twenty minutes after visiting hours begin, figuring his parents would want time with him first. I glance at my agent escort, a nice, but tough-looking woman who's filling in for Smirley, never thinking in a million years I'd need an armed bodyguard. Finding a place to park is already a challenge. We cruise down three aisles before spotting one. For the past fourteen hours, all I've wanted was to be in this building. To see him. To be near him. To feel the warmth rising in my cheeks when those ebony eyes peer into mine. And I thought maybe, if we catch a moment alone, our first kiss might even take place in this hospital. But as I enter the building, another emotion wraps around me like a choking weed.

Fear.

Because this could be the last straw. It would be completely reasonable for him to be done with all the drama, all the life-threatening situations and cops and bad guys and FBI. So maybe what I'll find when I enter room 229 and walk to Bed 2, is someone who's just done with *me*. I shake my head, knowing I couldn't blame him one bit. Wishing we'd just had the chance to have one date at Little Italian. Or anywhere.

As we approach the room, Agent Rojas stops at the door. "I'll wait out here." Like Smirley, her signing is flawless. Guess that's why they chose her for me.

"Okay, thanks. I won't be long."

An empty bed greets me as I enter the room, but a jacket and purse lay on the chair beyond the divider curtain. Someone is here. Probably his parents, who are about to meet the girl responsible for their son lying in a hospital for the second time in three days. Indirectly, unknowingly, and certainly unwillingly, but that doesn't change the outcome. My feet threaten to turn around, but I force them forward, past the first bed, past the half-closed curtain.

Three sets of eyes turn my way. His mother sits on the edge of the bed, her dark eyes a reflection of Nathan's. His father stands by the window. Nathan sits at an angle, leaning against the partially upright bed. He says, "This is Haylie," signing as he speaks, though his lips are not difficult to read. I tense until they smile. Warm smiles. Sincere. Void of hate or blame. I smile back and wave, wondering what to do next, when Mrs. Boliva rises, walks over, and hugs me. Caught entirely off guard, I stiffen, then return the unexpected hug. Nathan squeezes his eyes shut and shakes his head as he signs, "Sorry."

When she pulls away, her eyes shimmer with emotion. She turns to Nathan and says something I can't see, then places her palms on my cheeks.

"She's happy you're safe," Nathan says.

I sign "thank you" and she removes her hands to gesture toward the spot where she'd been sitting. I shake my head, using the same gesture to tell her to sit there, but she insists by pointing to it again. I like her already.

Nathan takes my hand, casually, tenderly, as if it isn't the first time we've touched. As if it's perfectly normal. The warmth of his skin melts into mine and I try to act nonchalant despite a quickening of my pulse. When he tells his parents to face me so I can read their lips, his dad steps in front of me, scooting down so our faces are level with each other. It's a silly and unnecessary move, absolutely ridiculous, and yet...the sweetness of it nearly brings tears to my eyes. These are good people.

"We will leave so you two can talk." His words are slow and deliberate as he points to me and Nathan, then ends with the universal "okay" sign. "We will get coffee." This time he concludes with a mime to show he's drinking coffee. I stifle a laugh, hoping Nathan will explain he doesn't have to act out his words. I smile and offer another "thank you," appreciating his efforts and hoping I get the chance to see them again. Knowing it's not something to count on.

They walk out, and we are alone. Morning light streams in through the window, illuminating his bandaged shoulder in a sunbeam. I stare at it, forgetting all the words I'd imagined saying during the drive to the hospital. He raises his good arm to touch my cheek, and I shift my gaze to his face.

"Are you okay?"

I'm not. This whole thing has been terrifying and

awful, and seeing him like this reminds me that it's not done being awful. My family is stuck in a "secured location," living in fear that some maniac will do whatever it takes to get Mom's laptop. Or just get Mom - the only living human who knows that formula. And Nathan's sitting there damaged and broken, trying to veil his pain, and asking if *I'm* okay.

"No, because you're here. I'm sorry. You didn't deserve this."

"Neither did you. No apologies, okay? I'm happy you're safe. Sorry I can't sign for a while."

"It's fine. I'm good at reading lips." I keep my sentences simple, knowing he's still learning. "How bad is it?"

He tells me the bullet missed a major nerve bundle and something else that would have caused serious damage, but swim team is still a possibility for next year. They're releasing him tonight, but he won't be at school tomorrow. He asks about me and my family, and I tell him we're doing fine in the "secret hideout."

"I bet it's like the Bat Cave."

I laugh and shake my head. "Not even close." Despite our different languages, talking to Nathan is comfortable. Easy. Every moment with him makes me want to know him better. His dark eyes linger on mine like he feels the same way, and still I wait for the sky to fall. With all that's happened, there's no reason this guy should want anything to do with me.

He takes my hand. "I want to tell you something."

My insides slump. Here we go. "Okay."

"I was really looking forward to our date, then everything went south and turned into a mess."

I stop breathing, telling myself it will be all right. This poor guy needs to separate himself from all the insanity. He needs to heal. He needs a break. And I need to be okay with that.

"It may be a few days before I can go out. I have to

take some meds for a couple of days, and not move too much. Our first date might need to be at my house, if you're cool with that."

The words bounce around inside my head. Maybe I misinterpreted. "At your house?"

"Yes. I know, it's kind of lame, but – "

"Yes." My hand bobs the word so fast I probably look desperate, but I don't even care. He still wants to give this a shot, and I'm all in. His eyes tell me he's all in, too.

"Is Wednesday okay? After school?"

I nod. "Wednesday."

"Good."

He smiles. I smile. Awkwardness permeates the walls, the air, my pores. I search for something to say, drawing a blank despite all we've experienced in the past few days. I glance out the window for inspiration, desperate enough to comment on the weather, which isn't particularly noteworthy. The remains of his scrambled egg breakfast sit on a tray next to his bed. I decide to ask if it was good, but he touches my arm.

"Did you see Smirley in the halls?"

Nathan saves the day. He's been doing a lot of that; I need to step up. "No. I've got a different agent with me today. She's waiting by the door. Did Smirley come to question you again?"

"No, but he stopped in, dressed in regular clothes. It was weird to see him without the suit. He was visiting his wife and wanted to see how I was doing."

"Really? I'm not surprised, though. I thought he was nice, even though you said he was a jerk."

Nathan nods, laughing a little. "Yeah, but now I'm not so sure. Something crazy happened. He apologized. He said his wife has been here for two weeks and they don't know what's wrong with her. He's been very stressed. He admitted he sometimes took it out on me."

"Wow."

"I actually felt bad for the guy. Kinda weird, though.

He was here when you texted about coming to visit. When I told him, he had a strange expression and wanted to know what time…"

"That's odd. I wonder why."

Nathan leans toward the tray table and reaches for the water bottle, then stops and winces. I grab it for him, hating the pain that tenses his face. I ask if he needs anything else, but he says "No," then shifts his gaze left, where his parents are walking in with their coffee.

His mom points to her cup, wrinkles her nose and says, "Bad coffee." I laugh; she does the same. It's a nice moment, until I notice the wall clock. My visit here came at a price. I promised it would be short, and that I'd babysit this morning. I stand and slip my purse strap onto my shoulder. Mr. Boliva steps toward me again and says, "Please stay," in his overdramatized way to make it "easier" for me to understand. He's really trying. Tomorrow I'll tell Nathan to let them know they can speak normally.

I reach into my purse and text a message to Nathan without sending it. Instead, I show it to them.

Thank you, but I have to watch my little brother while my parents go out. They need me back by ten-thirty. It was really nice to meet you.

I scroll through my photos for a good one of Ben to show them. They smile and nod, with Mrs. Boliva saying Ben is "so cute, just like his sister." I hope she doesn't notice the heat rising to my cheeks. With goodbye waves and another quick hug from Nathan's mom, I head out to the hall, where Agent Rojas is waiting, then down to the lobby.

Sun pours down from a cloudless sky, promising a perfect autumn day. Red maples and golden aspens dot the parking lot, contrasting dramatically with the endless blue overhead. Maybe the darkness has come to an end. My heart smiles, replaying the scene where Nathan asks if I can visit him Wednesday. I don't know why he still wants to get together, given all that's transpired, but I'll take it.

We're nearly to the car when the air around me thickens. I stop, then continue forward while scanning the lot, futilely searching for...I don't even know what. But there's something. A heaviness. A presence in the atmosphere that casts an invisible shadow on this picture-perfect day. Maybe it's residual fear from the past few days, or lack of sleep from worrying about Nathan. Or maybe it's exactly what my instincts tell me is true.

I'm being watched.

My eyes take in the rows of cars, the brilliant trees, the signs, and people walking. A blond guy down the aisle glances away as I look toward him, quickly slipping into his car. The world around me looks just as it should. And yet my pulse throbs faster, my breaths come shorter, and an irrational fear crawls along the tiny hairs on the back of my neck. Ghostly visions of that night haunt my memory. The car vibrations, the men, the struggle, the ties and blindfold. This is different, though. It's daytime, with people everywhere and plenty of distance between me and that guy. And though I didn't get a look at his face, he clearly wasn't wearing a mask. If only that made his presence less sketchy.

Breathe, Haylie. You're fine.

Agent Rojas pauses by the car. "What's wrong?"

"I don't know. Just a weird feeling." She probably thinks I'm crazy.

"Get in." She closes the door behind me and walks slowly around the car, perusing the lot with her hand on her holstered gun, then gets in and locks the doors.

"I didn't see anything. Are you okay?"

"Yes. I'm probably just paranoid from everything that's happened."

"I put a lot of faith in people's instincts." She starts the car. "Believe me, listening to your instincts can save your life."

One more scan of the lot tells me there's nothing to fear, but facts and fear are seldom partners. As we head toward the exit, I glance in the rearview and see two cars behind us. It's fine. Twenty minutes from now I'll be back in my "secure location" playing Monopoly Junior with Ben and drinking hazelnut coffee. But as we stop at a traffic light, Agent Rojas gets a call that unsettles me. She only has three responses: "Where? How many?" and after a pause, "Got it." When the light turns green, she glances into the rearview mirror and takes off at a faster pace. I don't want to distract her by signing, but those instincts she mentioned tell me we are no longer safe.

I draw in a breath and try to remember what "safe" feels like.

———

My head sinks into the pillow, thankful this long day has come to an end. Visiting Nathan, entertaining Ben, hanging out with Imani, then physics and AP history. I turn from my back to my side, then back again, but my stiff neck and shoulders can't get comfortable. Maybe Mom's right about the stress taking a toll on all of us. She's had a headache all day, Ben's been cranky, and Dad yelled at the jaguar when we were at Wild Things. We're safe in this apartment, though. At least, that's what I try to tell myself so I'll fall asleep. I stare at the ceiling fan, barely visible in the darkness, when Ben comes in and grabs my arm.

This can't be good.

He flips on the light. "Phone just rang. Something's going on."

I toss back the covers and we fly to the living room, where Mom is on the phone and Dad's on the couch, listening.

"What's happening?"

"Something about Steve," Dad says. "It sounds like he was stalking you. Wait." He turns toward Mom.

I do the same, but her lips are partially blocked by the receiver. She looks at me, eyes glistening. "They got him! And the other guys, too. The ones who wanted to buy the formula." Mom listens another minute and turns to us again. "And they rescued the little boy. He's okay." She talks a few more minutes and hangs up, then joins us on the couch.

"He shot Nathan because he figured you'd visit him today at the hospital. He planned to follow you back here, then break in to get the formula, or *me*. He had two guns and a stun gun on him. He was ready for anything."

It's painfully easy to imagine the horrific scene that would have played out if Steve had his way. What if Ben got shot? Or *any* of us? My head finds it impossible to wrap around a level of greed that negates the precious, immeasurable value of human life.

"But Smirley felt like something was wrong. He stayed in the lobby, waiting for you and the agent to leave, then followed you out of the parking lot. When Smirley saw Steve, he alerted Agent Rojas and called for backup, then followed Steve. If Smirley hadn't been there...if he hadn't seen you..."

Her hands cover her mouth and she squeezes her eyes shut. I wait for her to finish the sentence, but then I see it. Her hands are trembling. Her whole body is trembling. Tears slip through eyelashes pressed closed and trickle down her face. Dad moves to hold her but I beat him to it, wrapping my arms around her shoulders. My strong mom, my hero, who has faced struggles with grace and courage, crumbles in my arms. I want to tell her it's okay, that we're safe now, that she doesn't need to cry, and that I love her to the moon and back, like she always says to me. But I don't want to pull away. My arms remain in place and I say it all...without speaking a word.

Chapter 21

Nathan
Monday Afternoon

Cougar races after the stick, his greyhound legs easily outrunning it, then turns and leaps, catching it like a champ. Alec laughs, every time, and calls him back for more. If it weren't for this messed-up shoulder, I never would have known such a simple thing would bring my friend so much joy. Or maybe he's just happy to be skipping school.

A cool breeze bends the grass in the field as Cougar races back. He's loving the attention, especially after too much time cooped up in the house the past few days. I stand in the field, feeling the warmth of the sun on my face and smiling at the sight of Cougar leaping through the overgrown prairie grass. I take a few steps to catch up to Alec. "I still can't believe your dad told you to ditch school today."

"Crazy, right? But it's been a weird weekend. Insane, actually."

Alec is different. There's no describing how; no explaining why I think so, but it's there in his voice, his movements. The way he carries himself. It's something incredibly subtle and blatantly obvious. Whatever it is, it's good. That's all that matters.

He flings the stick again and my crazy greyhound bolts after it, nearly becoming a blur. "And we talked about some things. I don't know, maybe that had something to do with it."

"Things like?"

He shrugs. "You know, just things."

I don't know, but he's going to tell me before this day is out. I feel it. Cougar comes racing toward me with his prize, and I brace, knowing he's going to leap and there is absolutely going to be pain. He jumps, and Alec steps in front of me, blocking the attack.

"Impressive. Thanks." I watch him take the stick from Cougar and whip it back into the field. "You may be doing this awhile. Doc says it could be six months before I can throw again."

"I'll do it every day," he says. "I don't mind a bit."

"I can see that."

"You'll be going to physical therapy, then?"

The wind catches a bunch of fallen leaves and they swirl in front of us like a tiny tornado.

"Yeah, I'm already booked for the next six Saturday afternoons." The thought of therapy exhausts me. In fact, just standing here is starting to wear me down. Maybe it's the meds, or the energy that gets sucked up in the healing process. I'm way too young to feel this old.

Cougar returns, jumping on Alec, who grabs the stick for another toss. "Saturdays, huh?"

"Yep." *Come on, Alec. You're almost there. Tell me where you go.*

"Saturdays." Alec disappears on me for a moment. There's a distant look in his eyes. To Cougar's dismay, he holds on to the stick instead of tossing it. A nudge from my pup brings him back to the here and now. He throws the stick and turns to me, eyes narrowing. "You okay? You look a bit knackered."

"It's the pain meds. They drag me down. I'm not taking

them after today."

"Let's rest a bit." He points to a bench by the trees and we head over, with Cougar trailing close behind. It feels good to relax on the wooden slats. My pup circles a patch of grass three times before curling up with his crazy long front legs flopped over his back legs like a misshapen pretzel. I start to lean back, but the position sends pain darting through my shoulder, so I sit soldier straight and wait for my friend to unveil whatever's weighing on his mind.

Alec sighs. Says nothing. Sighs again.

A hawk soars overhead, rising, dipping, then disappears over the rooftops. A mom and toddler cross the field. She picks him up and swings him around before they continue on their way. Still, my friend stays quiet. I consider saying something to nudge him along but decide not to break his contemplation.

He picks up a long blade of grass and tears it into tiny pieces, then does the same with a leaf.

And still he's silent. And still I wait.

He closes his eyes. "There was a spider."

"I know." Unexpected, but however he wants to lead into this is fine with me. "You killed it, though. Killed your phone, too. Nice job."

Eyes open. More waiting.

"The day Jenna died."

Silence permeates the air around us. No birds, no breeze rustling the leaves. Just...silence.

"I wasn't supposed to pick her up without permission. Or walk with her. Sometimes Mum would let me hold her on the couch. But that day, my sixth birthday, I wanted to show them I could do it. They were in the kitchen having tea when I went into her room and picked her up. Real gentle, you know." His arms curve around each other in front of him, like he's cradling his baby sister.

"I planned to call them over and surprise them when I'd reached the couch. I imagined how proud they'd be to see what a good job I did. How careful I was. It was summer. Hot. I was wearin' shorts and no shoes. Maybe if I was wearin' shoes or long pants, it wouldn't have happened. If I'd just stepped an inch to the left or right..."

His voice cracks. He stops talking.

"It's okay, Alec." My entire body tenses in preparation for the story I've waited forever to hear—and now dread.

"I was walkin' over the little area rug when I felt a tickle on my foot. I glanced down. A big, black spider raced up my leg. I jerked. The rug twisted around my foot or somethin' and I was falling. I don't know what happened." Alec covers his face with his hands. He says nothing.

I want to comfort him in some way - make it better – but don't know where to start. Maybe he just needs me to listen.

"And Jenna, she wasn't in my arms anymore. She was in the air and I couldn't do anything." He rests his hands in his lap as a tear slides down his cheek. Then another. "I hit the floor. She hit the stone fireplace. Head first. She never cried. She just lay there, silent. Forever silent."

Alec quietly dissolves. No sobs. Not a sound as years of shame and self-hatred flow out in muted streams.

Chills prickle my back and arms. None of the scenarios I'd imagined ever played out this way. A trip. A fall. A lifeless child. This is what defines him. He's spent a lifetime crushed beneath the leaden weight of that guilt, and I am powerless to help. A huge void fills my head where the perfect words should be forming. "You were a kid, Alec. Six. It was an accident."

"Stop." He shakes his head at words he's probably heard dozens of times. Words that can't do the only thing that matters – turn back time. "Please, don't."

We sit. Alec wipes his eyes, but the source of tears seems limitless. I reach over and pat his leg – a gesture neither of us have ever done, but it feels right. In my family, there would be hugging, even among friends, and

I'm grateful my culture is comfortable with affection. But that might cross the line for Alec. So I go with three pats and leave it at that, hoping it provides some small source of comfort. "I'm sorry." It's the only thing I can think of. "I'm sorry that happened to you. To both of you."

He nods and sniffs. "Jenna's world ended that day. Mine, too, in a way. Everything changed. Me. My parents. Cat was so good with me. Held me half the night while I cried." Alec swipes his cheeks, then wipes his hand on his jeans. His emotions are not lost on Cougar, who unfurls himself from his patch of grass and lays his head on Alec's lap. There's no way for him to know what Alec just said, or the impact Jenna's death had on his life. There's no way my goofy Cougar could know Alec's been lugging around an anchor of pain since he was just a kid. And yet, there he stands, quietly comforting Alec.

"My parents, they still loved me, I guess, but it wasn't the same. Everyone grew a little colder. That's the only way I know to describe it." He reaches over and wraps an arm around Cougar. "I hoped moving to America would make it all better, but that dark cloud followed us right across the ocean and just kept hangin' over our house."

Again, I search for something profound, only to come up blank. Another "I'm sorry" will just sound lame.

"Until Friday."

"Friday? But that's when everything happened." It doesn't make sense that any of this could have turned around on the day Haylie and I were rescued from that motel.

"It's also when my dad waited with me while the FBI was rescuing you. He closed the store, Nathan. *Closed* it and came to be with me. And I was freaking out because I thought you'd get killed, and so he started talking about things to distract me. He was nice; the nicest he's ever been. And so calm." He strokes Cougar's back and gets rewarded with a lick on his arm. "Then you got rescued and he came with me to the hospital. We talked some more in the waiting room. I told him about...some decisions I've made lately, and he didn't get mad. Just offered some advice, and it was pretty good, too."

I sit in awe, realizing this is the most Alec has opened up to me since I've known him. "That's good. Really good. I wish it hadn't taken 'til now, but it happened. That's what matters." I resist the urge to ask about the "decisions," and wait for him to continue.

"And then the craziest part – we talked about Jenna for the first time since...since she died. Later that night, we talked some more with Mum. Sometimes one of us would cry. It was hard. And good. And awful. But mostly amazing." Walls crumble as he speaks. "I can't explain it, but when I woke up the next morning, that cloud was gone. I mean, it wasn't rainbows and butterflies, but it was different. The air was lighter. And I think the therapy helped a bit in making that happen."

If getting held at gunpoint resulted in the Channing family bonding and communicating, then sign me up to do it again.

"That's pretty amazing. I mean, I know it was hard, but wow, sounds like you guys needed that. Maybe they could go with you to therapy."

"Yeah, they're coming this Saturday. My dad talking to a therapist. Can you picture it?"

I can't. "Not even a little. So, that's the Saturday mystery? Therapy? Why didn't you tell me?"

"It's complicated. I started going because of the arachnophobia. I have to learn how to deal with spiders."

"No wonder you didn't scream in the car. You settled down quicker than ever."

He shrugs. "It's definitely helping, but I still have a ways to go. I mean, there's going to be situations coming up where I can't freak out and apparently the spider issue is just a symptom of underlying problems. So I've been talking to the therapist about Jenna, my parents...and other things."

There it is again. He's told me so much already, but he's got something tucked away that's even harder than talking about Jenna.

"Good. I'm glad you're going. By the time we start college, you'll be a new man. Maybe the therapy will even help you figure out what you want to major in."

"Listen, mate, there's something— "

"And they have a Wilderness Club. I didn't mention it before, but if you get over the spider thing, maybe we could join and go – "

"Nathan!"

"What?"

"The therapy...it's only part of what I do on Saturdays."

Apprehension saturates our sunny little corner of the world. The wind whispers, *Hang on, Nathan, hang on tight, because something's about to knock you off this bench.*

"Listening."

"I work out with some guys. They're...they're..." He stops cold and stares off toward the horizon again.

Was I totally off base about the steroids? I look at the guy who's been my best friend for ten years, the heartthrob of Beethoven High with his shaggy black hair, easy smile, and flawless charm, and wonder if all the flirting and dating has been a façade. Could I have spent an entire decade not seeing the truth? Not seeing the real Alec? If I've been that oblivious, I need to do some serious soul searching.

"What? Gay? Are you going to tell me you're gay? Or bi? Because you know I don't care, right? Though I totally did *not* see this coming. Not even a hint. I mean, you and girls, right? You know it wouldn't change anything."

Alec shakes his head, smiling for the first time since we sat down. "Actually, it would change things *quite a lot*, because you're right, I'm all about the girls."

"I knew that."

"But, Nathan, these guys are, um—"

"What? Spit it out. You're killin' me." I wait, back to feeling certain it's steroids, and ready to recommend places he can get help. I've been preparing for this. I'll go with him, too, so he feels supported and doesn't ditch the appointments.

He sighs. "They're guys I enlisted with."

Enlisted. He's not making sense. I turn to him, but his eyes fixate on the grass, like there's something hidden in the field that will reveal itself if he stares hard enough. Enlisted. Odd word choice. Probably joined a gym with these guys, because he can't mean *enlisted*. We're starting college in ten months. I want to ask him what he means, but instead, I watch the geese mulling around the field, picking at grass. One gets mad at another and chases him, head low, neck stretched out. They run around the other geese, who squawk a little, then stop and go back to eating grass. I don't get geese.

Alec leans back against the bench. "Did you hear me?"

"Yeah." There's nothing else to say. If I ask about "enlisted," he'll answer, so I keep watching the geese.

"I'm not going to college with you, mate. I'm sorry. Really. I joined the Air Force."

A raging river of blood rushes into my head, pounding my eardrums. Alec joined the Air Force. Not going to college. Leaving Heron Lake. Leaving me. This isn't like trying a new kind of ice cream or taking a girl to someplace other than Café Luis. This is an earthquake shifting my entire foundation.

But that's what life does.

If I don't make changes, too, I'll end up watching the grass grow and spying on neighbors from the safety of my living room. I'll delight in pulled pork "sammiches" with coleslaw and worry about dogs stepping on the lawn. This is happening, and I need to let it happen. Be supportive. Alec needs and deserves that.

I stare out at the invisible divide between knowing the

right thing to do and actually acting on it. "Oh. Wow. Congratulations, or whatever."

"Basic training starts a few weeks after graduation."

And now it has a timeline. I take a breath. Every molecule within me wants to scream at him, beg him to not to do it, tell him he's crazy. But I will do this. For Alec. And for myself, as well. "When did you enlist?"

"About a month ago. I know, I know, you're going to say I should have told you, and I wanted to. Really. But every time I planned it, I'd chicken out. It never felt right."

And that's on me. Because telling your best friend anything should always feel right. But Alec knew, after years of seeing me stay in my safe zone, stick with the predictable, the familiar, that this would unravel me.

Cougar lifts his head from Alec's lap, takes a step and lays it on mine. Everything I'd imagined the next few years would be has just imploded. But all along, it was *my* vision. What *I* wanted, not just for me, but for Alec, too. And I never stopped to consider he needed to figure out his own life.

"You okay?" Alec reaches over to pet Cougar. "I know this is kinda huge."

"It is. Really huge."

"I'm sorry."

He's spent far too much of his life being sorry. He needs to know I'll be okay.

"For having a life? For choosing to serve our country? You need to make your own way. Do your own thing. I'm the one who's sorry. Change isn't my best thing, but that needs to, you know, change."

He laughs. "Well said. Thanks."

"Life is short. Kinda fragile, too. You don't need someone controlling it." I pet Cougar, drawing comfort from his compassion.

"You never did that."

"Not intentionally, maybe, but I made assumptions. I

figured what was best for me was best for you."

Cougar licks my hand. "I'm all right, boy." I look at my dog, thinking how weird it must be for him to be out here without his friend, and realize Alec wasn't the only one impacted by my fear of change. "I'm doing the same thing with Ruby."

"I know. It's okay. Really tough thing to do."

I shake my head. It most definitely is not okay. "I'm letting her suffer because I want her alive. Because a world without Ruby is too hard of a change for *me*." My Ruby girl. This is going to wreck me. "What are you doing tomorrow after school?"

"Stoppin' by to steal a Pop Tart, then workin' on that *Farenheight 451* paper for Wednesday." His pantry is full of the best baked treats in town, but to Alec, nothing beats a Pop Tart.

"Maybe first we could take a ride."

He nods. "The vet?"

I open my mouth to say "yes," but no words emerge past the lump.

"I got you, mate. It's gonna be hard for me, too. I love that dog, but we'll do this. Your Ruby, she'll be better off. You know that, right?"

I nod, still unable to speak.

"You okay?"

"Yeah, fine." We both know that's a lie, but I'll get my act together and do it. I have to. For my girl.

Chapter 22

Nathan
Wednesday -one week after the kidnapping

The great blue heron steals silently through the shallows, leaving no ripples behind as he seeks his prey. Haylie and I watch from the deck. Death comes soon to the unsuspecting fish that cross his watery path. The heron stops, extending his sleek, feathery neck over the water, motionless as a lion hiding in the savannah grass. He is truly king of the lake. Even the occasional fox and coyote know better than to mess with his beak of death.

Except for the breeze ruffling his feathers, he could be an ice sculpture at one of those fancy buffets. He takes a step forward and freezes again. Haylie tenses. And then...the kill! He strikes and captures a small silvery carp. It wiggles from both sides of that five-inch dagger. But King Heron's not into a moving dinner. He drops it on the rocks, stabbing once, then twice, and the fish lies still, the late afternoon sun glinting on its scales for the last time. The heron tosses it until the carp slides headfirst down its throat. Hunger satiated, it flaps away toward the cattail marsh.

Haylie squeezes my hand. Her eyes tell me she's awed by the brutal beauty of the feast. A white gull skims the water, then heads skyward with a screech. A cool breeze shimmers across pink water reflecting an awesome autumn sunset. All of creation is showing off for Haylie.

We leave our patch of grass under the willow and head for the rocks, where the empty throne waits for us. There is room enough for two if you sit very, very close. We do. Jeans against jeans, jackets pressed together. The rock is cold and uncomfortable, but neither of us cares. A small wind blows wisps of that silky wheat hair onto my cheek. I turn to face her, breathing in the scent of soap and lilac and pure Haylie. My brain goes into sensory overload, but it's nothing compared to the feel of her warm lips on mine. We kiss again…and again. I wait for that awkward moment that follows a first kiss, but Haylie's steady gaze and confident smile form a force field that awkward can't break through.

I lean in for more, hopelessly lost in her eyes, anxious to learn everything about her. And wanting to never, ever, be farther away from her than I am right now. And as we sit, completely absorbed in each other, laughter draws our attention to the lake path. We turn to see Mr. Kingman strolling hand in hand with Mrs. Vitalli. In the other hand, he holds Lily's leash. The little spaniel barks at a goose family and they waddle away, voicing their indignation with honks and grunts.

Kingman sees me and let's go of Mrs. Vitalli, waving with a sweeping motion like he's signaling a rescue plane. "Hey there, Nathan!" he calls, then grasps her hand again.

Yes, Mr. Kingman, I see you standing there with your girlfriend and your little dog and your new life. "Hi, Mr. K., Mrs. Vitalli."

"Hello, Nathan." Mrs. Vitalli's singsong voice travels down the path and reaches me with a smile. They draw closer. "Who's your friend?"

"Haylie."

"Oh, my. The Haylie from the news?"

I translate for her and she turns toward them with a

friendly wave.

Mrs. Vitalli returns the gesture. "PLEASE TELL HER I'M SO HAPPY SHE GOT RESCUED."

Her words blast about twenty decibels higher than normal, like that's going to compensate for Haylie's lack of hearing. It's hard not to crack up, but you gotta love her. "I will." My hands begin to send the message, but Haylie stops me halfway, flashing them a princess smile with her response.

"She says thank you."

"She's a real gem, Nathan," Mr. Kingman whispers, which has as much effect on Haylie as the shouting. "Pretty as a picture. Brave, too. You better hold on to that one."

"Will do, Mr. K., and don't forget we're going out for pulled pork sandwiches tomorrow."

"Yes, yes! With the coleslaw on top!" He gives me a thumbs-up as they continue down the path, leaves floating around them like a scene out of a Hallmark movie. Some hit the water, gliding away like little elf boats. Others drift into Mr. Kingman's backyard, where they'll likely be attacked by his angry rake at the crack of dawn. But no, this is a new season for Mr. Kingman. Maybe the leaves will rest in peace.

Ahead of them lies Alec's house, and just beyond is the marshy area where the cattails are fading from green to gold. Haylie and I didn't have time to walk that far today, but she said she wants to next time.

Next time. My favorite new phrase. Please let there always be a next time.

She leans away from me, just far enough so her hands have room to move.

"There is something I never told you. I was terrified in that motel room. For a few minutes, I thought you were dead."

I'd used the time stuck at home to work on my signing skills. Still not great, but better than before. "Same. I thought that guy was going to strangle you and I couldn't do anything but watch. Nothing in my life has ever felt that horrible."

I don't tell her that yesterday was a close second. Holding Ruby until she took her last breath, with Alec at my side. Sobbing like a child over her lifeless body. But even then, I knew it was right.

She places warm palms on either side of my face, those hazel eyes saying more than words. With a flip of her hair, she moves her hands to speak again. "We made it, Nathan. I don't think we'll ever be the same, but that's okay. I see things differently now, don't you?"

I nod. "Definitely."

Facing death gave me a new set of eyes. I see life as a river now, ever changing, bending, flowing peacefully, churning into rapids. And sometimes deceptively calm on the surface while a deadly rip current surges beneath. Traversing the unpredictable waters is all about how you respond. Where to turn for guidance, when to go with the flow and when to navigate. And sometimes, fighting the undertow with everything you've got.

"I'm glad it's over." She leans her head on my shoulder, and even though it's my good shoulder, it still makes the injured one ache - a welcome sacrifice for the pure bliss of having no space between us.

I wrap my arm around her, wishing I could do the same with the other arm. For now, I'll happily stay here holding Haylie until I'm Kingman's age. Maybe older. All too soon, Haylie's phone vibrates and my plan unravels. She raises her head to check the caller ID, then points to the illuminated "Dad" on her screen. He's waiting out front to take her home. Nice guy, as it turns out, but I'm less than thrilled with his timing.

"I don't want to go." She sets her phone on her lap, lips pursed in a frown as she watches a family of ducks slip into the water.

She wants to stay. I hope that happens, but even if it

doesn't...she *wants* to. "Ask if you can stay longer."

As she turns to me, the breeze catches her hair, blowing it behind her as the sunset casts a golden glow on her face. Everything inside me melts.

"My grandparents are coming," she says. "We're going to Café Luis. I love that place."

I *knew* she was perfect. Wait 'til I tell Alec. "Do you want to go there Friday, too, instead of Italian Village?"

"No. Picturing us there helped keep me sane during the kidnapping."

I know that picture backward and forward. Me and Haylie at a little wooden table with the fake candle pushed to the side to make room for a gooey, steaming deep-dish pizza. Soft Italian music in the background. Walls covered with murals of the Colosseum, ancient ruins, grapes and vineyards. In the middle of the chaos, that vision kept me moving forward. Held a promise of better things to come. Gave me hope. "Ditto."

Hand in hand, we walk to the car and say goodbye. Her stepdad nods a greeting, then grabs his phone and pretends to read messages. Yeah, he's pretty cool. In his shoes, I probably would have suspected me, too. And hated my guts. But that's history. Haylie's here now, safe, standing next to me and wishing she could stay. And Friday, if the universe cooperates, we'll finally have our pizza. Not a particularly lofty goal for most people, but to us, nothing short of a miracle.

About the Author

Faith, family, and a passion for nature, writing, and photography nurture Susan's soul. She loves to visit the world's amazing places and has a travel bucket list that includes seeing the Northern Lights, the wild horses of the Outer Banks, and New Zealand's glowworm caves.

Susan worked as a Chicago-area newspaper reporter, then as a television reporter in Albuquerque before returning to her home state of Illinois. She currently works in public relations, teaches writing workshops, and gives travel presentations throughout the Chicago suburbs. Susan is president of the American Christian Fiction Writers Chicago chapter and a member of the Society of Children's Book Writers and Illustrators.

Acknowledgments

Huge thanks to all those who helped me shape the characters of Haylie, Nathan, Alec, and even Ruby and Cougar; to those whose eagle eyes spotted spelling and grammar errors; and for all the insight that helped forge the plot and subplots of this book.

I am immensely grateful to:

God, for everything good in my life, including the ability to write and the opportunity to make a living at it.

Dawn Carrington, Vinspire Publishing's Editor-in-Chief, for letting me share my imaginary friends with the world.

Gary Miura, whose decades of experience in law enforcement afforded plausibility to my crime scenes.

Patt Nicholls, for catching mistakes, offering suggestions, and cheering me on.

Schaumburg High School student Alexandra Rojas, for her Peruvian insight on Nathan's character and the storyline in general.

John Hersey High School students Belinda Lopez and Brianna Finnegan, both members of the Deaf Community, for their insight on Haylie's character and the storyline in general.

And Melissa Swanson, Deaf/Hard of Hearing Program Administrator with the Northwest Suburban Special Education Organization and Pamela Wechman-Mueller, Deaf/Hard of Hearing Teacher at John Hersey High School, for their support and for serving as liaisons with some of my awesome beta readers.

Dear Reader

If you enjoyed reading *Signs in the Dark*, I would appreciate it if you would help others enjoy this book, too. Here are some of the ways you can help spread the word:

Lend it. This book is lending enabled so please share it with a friend.

Recommend it. Help other readers find this book by recommending it to friends, readers' groups, book clubs, and discussion forums.

Share it. Let other readers know you've read the book by positing a note to your social media account and/or your Goodreads account.

Review it. Please tell others why you liked this book by reviewing it on your favorite ebook site.

Everything you do to help others learn about my book is greatly appreciated!

Susan Miura

Plan Your Next Escape!
What's Your Reading Pleasure?

Whether it's captivating historical romance, intriguing mysteries, young adult romance, illustrated children's books, or uplifting love stories, Vinspire Publishing has the adventure for you!

For a complete listing of books available, visit our website at www.vinspirepublishing.com.

Like us on Facebook at
www.facebook.com/VinspirePublishing

Follow us on Twitter at
www.twitter.com/vinspire2004

and follow our blog for details of our upcoming releases, giveaways, author insights, and more!

www.vinspirepublishingblog.com.

We are your travel guide to your next adventure!